Woodland Press Presents

LEGENDS
OF
THE MOUNTAIN
STATE

Edited By Michael Knost

Dedication

In memory of Bill Marino, my fifth grade
teacher who introduced me to worlds beyond imagination and encouraged me to
make the most of this one.

PUBLISHED BY
Woodland Press, LLC

Chapmanville, West Virginia
Printed In The United States of America

What Others Are Saying About Legends Of The Mountain State

"When it seems like every genre anthology released these days tries to convince readers that it and it alone is reinventing the wheel, *Legends of the Mountain State: Ghostly Tales from the State of West Virginia* is more than a breath of fresh air; it's a testament to the power of traditional, simple story-telling. Editor Michael Knost has assembled thirteen elegant, eerie, and affecting ghost stories written by authors who know and respect the tradition of such tales, and each offers up an atmospheric, straightforward, uncluttered narrative that one can easily imagine being told around a campfire late at night, as the stars blink down their light from a cold heaven and the sounds beyond the fire become unnervingly semi-human. There is poetic elegance in such simplicity, and this outstanding anthology proves it over and again. *Simply superb.*"

—Bram Stoker and International Horror Guild Award-winner Gary A. Braunbeck, author of *The Cedar Hill Stories* and *Mr. Hands*

"Haunting and darkly beautiful, with atmosphere like a mist around every story. A spooky, enjoyable read. These writers capture the wry humor and the mournful ghosts of the region, and these tales follow you long after you've closed the book."

—Mary SanGiovanni, author of *The Hollower*

"The Appalachian Mountains will never be the same!"

—James Gunn, 2007 Grandmaster of Science Fiction

"West Virginia is a haunted land, rich with the old, old things that trouble and thrill us to our very souls. The mute wraiths wandering lonesome country roads, monsters from the bowels of the earth, and restless victims of murder or misadventure that fill the pages of *Legends of the Mountain State* call out our deepest fears and remind us that we're only flesh and blood—no match for the enduring ghosts of the past."

—Laura Benedict, author of *Isabella Moon*

"Burke, Hughes, Nassise, Justice, Green and Walters, dazzling gems in this chest of many treasures. Old and new voices alike, make *Legends of the Mountain State* an anthology not to be missed."

—Fran Friel, author of the Bram Stoker Award nominated, *Mama's Boy*

www.woodlandpress.com

FOREWORD

Walk into any bookstore in any state and go to the "local interest" section. Chances are you'll see at least a handful of books about supernatural and unexplained events in the area. All of them—from "Hauntings in Maine" to "Ghosts of Florida's Gulf Coast" to "California Horrors"—will claim that their state is "the most haunted state in the union."

Fact is, we're a haunted species. We populate wherever we live with all manner of ghosts, goblins, and ghouls.

Now, with this collection, West Virginia stakes its claim as one of if not the most haunted state in the Union.

Living as I do in good ole' New England, my first reaction is one of doubt and maybe a bit of defensiveness. After all, New England is home to the Salem witches, buried pirate gold, and ghostly shipwrecks.

After perusing the contents of this book, I may have to revaluate my opinion.

West Virginia has all the necessary ingredients for ghostly doings—small towns and isolated farms, coalmines that plunge deep into the bowels of the earth, lonely hollows and mountains, and—of course—superstitious people.

When it comes right down to it, we're *all* superstitious people, but I doubt any other state can claim anything as truly bizarre as the Point Pleasant "Mothman" (about which contributors, Thomas Monteleone and Joseph Nassise, know a thing or two). And any state that has experienced the Greenbrier Ghost—where in a court of law the word of a ghost actually helped solve a crime—or the bizarre hauntings in the Lowe Hotel, or the ghost of Mamie Thurman might actually be able to say it's the most haunted area in the country.

The book you are holding in your hands contains a wealth of ghostly doings, all of them based on "real" events. And in all of them, the eerie side of West Virginia was the springboard.

As much as it pains this old New Englander to say it, judging by this book, West Virginia quite possibly could be the *most* haunted state in the Union.

Rick Hautala
Master of contemporary horror and suspense

Westbrook, Maine
http://rickhautala.com

TABLE OF CONTENTS:

INTRODUCTION

Ghost stories and unexplained legends have circulated American townships and cities for centuries—none more so than those located along the beautiful Appalachian mountains.

One of the most storied states in this region is West Virginia. The state broke away from Virginia during the American Civil War and was admitted to the Union on June 20, 1863. It is the only state formed as a direct result of the Civil War. And the war itself became fodder for many of these legends and tales.

As the state's population grew, so did the number of legends and ghost sightings. In fact, some of the nation's scariest tales have originated from small town farms, coalmines, and hollows of the Mountain State.

The thirteen tales you are about to read are more than just documented biographies of legends, ghosts, or events. These are individual cases as told by some of the best storytellers in the business.

Welcome to a side of the Mountain State you've never traveled.

Michael Knost
Editor
Logan, West Virginia

Thomas F. Monteleone
IMAGES IN ANTHRACITE

Thomas F. Monteleone is a 4-time winner of the Bram Stoker Award, the highest honor for writers in the horror genre. He has written television scripts for *American Playhouse*, George Romero's *Tales from the Darkside*, and a series on Fox TV entitled *Night Visions*. He is also the author of the bestseller, *The Complete Idiot's Guide to Writing a Novel*.

It started for Cort when he got the letter.

Mr. Cortney Fallon
POB 2030
Parkton MD 21120

It took me a while to track you down, but I figured you might want to know about the things that are happening here and because they are affecting my life and my family's, and maybe yours, too. We've been renting this place for more than a year now and we think the ghost we're seeing is your father. Call me at the number at the bottom of the page and we can talk about this. If you're not concerned, maybe you ought.

Yours truly,
Calvin Hoetzel

Two lines on the upper left corner of the envelope read,

12 Lick Hollow Lane
Overton, West Virginia

Cort knew the address.

It had been the location of his parents' house and the place where he'd grown up until his father died. He'd been ten years old, and things had happened fast after that. His mother sold the house, and they moved north to a small town in Maryland called Glyndon where they lived with his Aunt Rae, his mom's older sister.

That had been thirty-two years ago. Enough time for a lot to have happened—like graduating from Towson University with a degree in communications, marrying a local girl from Baltimore, and watching their two kids grow up to start the college grind themselves. He'd been luckier than a lot of his friends because his marriage had been a pretty good one, and he didn't see it changing for the worse. He and Amy liked each other, did some things together and some things apart, and were living a pretty good life.

She had slipped into the internet auction business back when she needed to be home with the kids and had grown it into something viable and profitable. Cort lucked into a few positions when cable television was a new and strange business, getting him in on the ground floor. He went from lugging cables in and out of trailers at Orioles games to an assistant cameraman, eventually to Chief Camera, to Producer, to his present slot as Director of Sports Programming for the Mid-Atlantic Region. It helped that he liked sports and didn't mind the travel.

He'd been living an ordinary, but satisfying life. Until he got this goofy letter.

* * *

"What're you going to do about it?" said Amy as she sat down at the umbrella table on their backyard deck.

"I don't know. Call him, I guess." Cort looked out on the lawn where the pressure-treated swing-set and playhouse still occupied the yard's farthest corner. Trees and shrubs had overtaken it, and it looked like the skeletal remains of a frontier town long forgotten. He'd been meaning to dismantle the stuff for years, but something sentimental and deep inside had kept him from getting it done. It was like the final statement your kids aren't kids anymore.

Amy sighed. "You'd better be careful. He sounds like a nut."

"Well, he *could* be. I've already started checking on things. Larry has a couple of buddies in some DC law firm, they made a few calls to some of *their* friends . . ."

Amy nodded, picked up her glass of iced tea and sipped. Then: "They find anything yet?"

"A little. The house is owned by a guy named Davis Stemper, and he rents it out to Hoetzel, the guy who wrote the letter. I have a phone number on Stemper, but that's it, so far."

Amy leaned back in her chair, looked at me. "I'd call him. Now."

* * *

"Calvin? He seems like an all right person," said Davis Stemper.

From his voice, he sounded like he was in his forties, educated and easy-going. He volunteered to Cort he was a real estate broker in the nearby town of Beckley and owned a bunch of properties in the surrounding towns.

"Did you know anything about him seeing ghosts in your house?"

"Nope, you callin' is the first I heard."

"What about people who've lived there before? Anybody else ever say they saw anything weird?"

Stemper paused, whistled softly for a moment. "Well, people down this way are a little superstitious, you know? I guess a few of 'em have said they've seen stuff."

"Stuff?"

"Yeah."

Cort waited for him to elaborate, but it didn't seem like it was going to be forthcoming. So: "Stuff in *your* house?"

"Yeah, I guess you could say that."

Sensing Mr. Davis Stemper didn't have a flair for detail or narrative, Cort said his thanks and goodbyes and keyed out the call. Other than a fair assurance Calvin Hoetzel was not a psychotic killer, Cort hadn't learned much. He had to make the choice to either ignore the whole deal or do something about it.

He picked up the latter and kicked things into motion by driving over to Kevin's place. Edgar Kevin Fitzsimmons was his actual name, but nobody since high school had ever called him anything but Kevin. He once tried to start a campaign urging everyone to call him *EK,* but everybody thought it was dopey and annoying. Without putting too fine a point on it, Kevin could be very odd, but that trait was more than mitigated by his amazing intellect and loyal friendship.

Kevin was one of those guys who managed to keep the not-getting-married thing fresh. Well, no, *fresh* wasn't exactly right, thought Cort. Maybe *believable*. The reason Kevin had remained single into his early forties was simple—he was too *weird* to interest almost *any* woman who wanted a husband. Kevin had been the only child of two brilliant parents—dad had been a physicist at Johns Hopkins Applied Labs and mom had been second violin with the BSO. Consequently, they left him alone a lot. And being a pretty brilliant kid himself, Kevin perused many of the thousands of books in the family home and developed an eclectic range of interests: local college and pro sports, silk screen printing, music, marine biology, paranormal investigation, gourmet cooking, real estate, eBay, and playing lots of golf. These were some of his primaries, but there were lots of others. He was one of those guys who didn't know a little bit about everything—he knew *a lot* about everything. But in his areas of interest, he was downright encyclopedic. Overlay all this with a touch of obsessive-compulsive personality, plus a stunningly original sense of humor, and you've got an original piece of work.

Kevin lived in a nice townhouse in an area south of Baltimore called Ellicott City, and he kept it in what he called *protoantiseptic* condition. Everything was always neat, always clean. Enough shelves, storage racks, bookcases, and containers to open an Ikea branch. He spent a lot of time organizing, alphabetizing, and fiddling with his stuff.

He also liked to while away the hours by making lists. One time, while they were watching a Ravens game, Cort found a legal pad with more than seventy entries written in a small, fevered script—the first one was "Cheerios" and the last one was "Post Toasties." Kevin had been wondering just exactly how many cereals he could name. . . .

Yeah, Kevin would be the only guy who could help with this one. The thought both comforted and amused Cort as he pushed Kevin's doorbell.

* * *

After Cort quickly reprised the letter and phone call, Kevin rescued a couple of Rolling Rocks from the kitchen, and the two of them retreated to a backyard patio slightly larger than a commemorative postage stamp.

"So, whaddya think? What should I do?" Cort eased into one of the Adirondack chairs.

Kevin smiled. "Well, you know my basic problem with ghosts?"

"I didn't know you had one, but no, what is it?"

"I think all ghosts should be *naked*. I mean, how come people always see them in their *clothes*? Cotton and nylon have an afterlife? I don't think so."

Cort nodded. "Good point. Which pretty much means ghosts are BS, right?"

"That would be too easy," said Kevin. "No, my gut tells me people are seeing *something*, but it might not be what we think it is. And good thing, too. If my grandmother visited right after she died, I'm pretty sure I wouldn't want the no-clothes thing working, you know?"

"Yeah, you have a point," said Cort. "Got any ideas?"

"Sure," he said just before tilting back the rest of the green glass bottle. "As usual, I've always got plenty of 'em. You've heard of the 'residual' phenomenon, right?"

Cort shrugged. He was mildly interested in the paranormal and watched stuff on the Discovery Channel if he stumbled on it. But it was all part of his general curiosity about the world, rather than any special interest in ghosts. So he said, "A little, I guess. Refresh my memory."

Kevin nodded. "Okay, some people think certain places can act like recording devices, and certain images kind of get captured there and they get replayed over and over. They call them residual images."

Cort smiled. "That sounds so . . . so convenient."

"Why? Because it explains what's going on?"

"I was thinking more of the mechanism involved," said Cort. "Does anybody explain exactly *how* these recordings happen or, hey . . . get played back? I mean, c'mon, where's the *rewind* button?"

Kevin held up an index finger, as though making an important point. "We don't have all the details worked out yet."

"We?"

"The editorial 'we.' I just identify with that vast legion of ghost hunters who want the truth—whatever it is. And the residual thing, well, it does explain why ghosts aren't naked."

Cort thought about this. "It also, to me at least, says they aren't really *ghosts*. Any more than a PowerPoint presentation . . ."

Kevin looked at him, leaned back and arranged a smug expression. "If you really believed that, you wouldn't be sitting here talking about it."

Cort nodded. "Okay, so what should I do about it?"

"Let's go down there. Wouldn't it be great if we can see this guy who says he's your father?"

Although Cort didn't want to admit it, that was exactly

what he'd been hoping for. His memories of his father were dim and distant and not very well realized—just like his old photographs from the era when Kodak color film faded away with the years.

"Sounds like a plan," he said. "You sure you want to do this?"

Kevin stood, headed inside for two more Rocks. "Are you kidding? A chance to see a ghost? Or whatever it is. I'm there."

* * *

The drive down to Overton, West Virginia, took about ten hours, and Kevin used most of it to expound on his theories about the coming global superstorms and his continuing lament that he would not live long enough to enjoy personal jet-pack travel like the old sci-fi magazine covers by Frank R. Paul promised.

Cort hadn't spent this much continuous one-on-one time with Kevin since their college days, and he'd forgotten how funny and simultaneously draining he could be. His energy and sense of wonder was like a five-year-old's, but when they rounded the final hill leading into Overton, even Kevin succumbed to the essential *grimness* of the place.

"Oh man," he said. "Can you say *Ninth Circle*?"

Ahead of them, a claustrophobic smear of asphalt sank between a double row of two-story storefronts—faded asbestos shingles and dull paint. Dim, flyspecked windows and faded signs formed the backdrop for the funereal passage of round-shouldered pedestrians. Kevin drove his Volvo SUV down the center of the town's main thoroughfare as Cort felt a wave of recognition shudder through him like a blast of winter through an open door.

He had been a part of this place, had swept it from his memories, but it came back to him with a slap. He gave Kevin a series of left and right turns, and they were suddenly on Lick Hollow Lane in front of a house with a number 12 on a rusty mailbox.

Other than a few more trees, it was weird to see how *unchanged* everything was. His old house, an ugly two-story cube, looked pretty much the same as the day he and his mother had moved out all those years ago. Cort had imagined feeling something ominous when he finally saw it again, but in truth, he didn't feel much of anything.

"Real palace, huh?" he said.

Kevin shrugged. "Nobody gets to pick where they come from."

Having called ahead, Cort figured Calvin Hoetzel would be expecting them. He nodded to Kevin and they both exited the car in silence. Cort wanted to say something clever, but the words just weren't there.

* * *

The front door with peeling, dark blue paint swung back to reveal Calvin Hoetzel—short, skinny, and a face that looked like the protagonist of a thousand country ballads. He was probably in his thirties but thinning hair, a disappearing chin, and sun-weathered cheeks made him look twenty years older. He invited them into the front room furnished with a round throw rug, a couch that sagged in the middle, and two card table chairs. These were arranged in a vague semi-circle facing a small television that rested atop the dusty carcass of a much older console TV. No pictures on the wall, no knick-knacks. Calvin Hoetzel was not exactly living the high life.

Somewhere in the back of the house, a woman's voice mingled with the chatter and giggles of small children. Hoetzel directed Cort and Kevin to the couch, then he pulled up one of the folding chairs for himself.

"Get you guys a beer or somethin'?"

Kevin declined for both of them while Cort cast about for ways to open the conversation. He didn't have to because Hoetzel did it for him.

"You boys ever seen a ghost?"

Cort leaned forward. "No, and I gotta tell you, Mr. Hoetzel, I was shocked by your letter."

"I figured you might. But there was nothin' else I could do. That thing I've been seeing in here *told* me he needed to talk to his son. And he keeps saying it every time I see it."

"Can you describe what you see?"

Hoetzel nodded, pointed up at the ceiling. "Right upstairs. This guy dressed like a miner, he shows up in the middle of the night, in the middle of my bedroom. Then he disappears. Right in front of me. And he does it just about every night."

"And he speaks to you?" said Kevin.

Hoetzel nodded. "Yeah, he says he needs to tell his son, Cortney Fallon, what really happened."

"What really happened? What's he mean by that?"

"No idea." Hoetzel shrugged, then fumbled a pack of Marlboros out of his pocket, fired one up with a disposable lighter.

Kevin held up his hand as if in class. "Does he say it the same way every time?"

"Huh?" A plume of smoke followed this.

"Does it look like . . . I don't know . . . like you're watching a movie or something?"

"Yeah, I guess. Maybe."

Kevin nodded.

"I know this sounds crazy, but is there any way we could try to see this . . . ghost for ourselves?"

Hoetzel tilted his head towards the domestic sounds coming from the back of the house. "This place is all me and my family got."

Cort waved his hand. "I understand. But I have an idea . . . "

* * *

Three hours later, Cort and Kevin were sitting on those folding chairs, surrounded by the Spartan furnishings of the Hoetzels' bedroom. Kevin had a small LCD device that displayed the temperature in the room and an equally compact video recorder. Darkness was a great cloak, pierced by an occasional burst from Cort's mini maglite.

They were alone in the house as midnight ticked down upon them. When Cort had suggested a free weekend "vacation" in the nearby town of Beckley, Calvin Hoetzel and his wife didn't hesitate. Cort paid for a suite at the Courtyard Marriott, dinner, and tickets to the movies. The family would return sometime tomorrow after a round of miniature golf and a spin through the local arcade.

"You think this is for real?" Cort whispered.

"I don't know, but I sure hope so." Kevin swept the space in front of them with the external thermometer. They'd been sitting in the dark for an hour and had seen or heard nothing.

"I'm not sure what I want. This is starting to weird me out." Cort knew he'd get out of there in a heartbeat if Kevin suggested it.

Kevin nudged him. "Hey, what's that business about 'what really happened'? You have any idea what charmin' Cal was talking about?"

Cort exhaled slowly. "Not really. I can remember when my father died, it was in some kind of accident—what they always call a *mine disaster* around here."

"That's all you know?"

Cort shrugged. "My dad dug coal. The Pickman Mine is what it was called. Something happened and my father and some other miners were trapped. Some people seemed to think it was my father's fault."

Kevin shook his head slowly. "Oh man, you're kidding. Did you ever find out the details?"

"No, but when I was older, I pretty much figured that's why we moved out of town. I think everybody suddenly hated *us* for whatever my father did."

"Jeez, Cort, how come you never told me any of this?"

"It was a long time ago, and even back then, my mother did her best to keep it pretty vague."

Neither of them spoke for a minute or two, and the cold silence of the house seemed to grow thick around them.

Kevin checked the room temperature again. "So, wait a minute. You mean you never bothered to do a little checking around? You never Googled any Pickman Mine disasters or anything like that?"

"No, I honestly never did."

"Why?"

"Because there was something about the way my mother handled the whole thing—like none of it ever happened. I guess I respected her *need* to do it that way."

"Well, I hope you don't mind if I do a little nosing around when we get back."

"No, of course not, I wouldn't—"

"Whoa!" Kevin stood, held the thermometer out with his left hand. "You feel it get colder in here?"

Cort's arms suddenly goosebumped. Darn right he'd felt it. "What is it?"

Kevin stuffed the LCD in his pocket, palmed the video recorder, flicked it on. "Something's happening. You feel it?"

Just as he said that, a faint glow formed in the center of the room, like a luminous fog. Cort watched as the mist assumed the vague shape of a man, hunched over, immobile, as if locked within the wrestling hold of an unseen opponent. There was something about the position that disturbed Cort deeply. He could not see the man's face clearly, but he knew from memory and old photographs he was looking at his father, and he *knew* he was looking at him at the moment of his death.

"Oh, God. . ." Kevin whispered. "I hope I'm getting this."

Just as he said this, there came a sound of heavy breathing and a voice thin as if funneled through an antique phonograph.

"What's he saying?" said Cort. He could hear words but indistinctly, and just below the level of intelligibility.

What was happening here? The dimensions of the room seemed to be closing down, filling him with an intense feeling of claustrophobic terror, and while he had no way of verifying it, time itself seemed to be stretching out and sagging away from him like pulled taffy. As he strained to hear the long, unending stream of words from the translucent phantom, he fought against an odd, intoxicating wave of fear and elation. Somehow, he knew he had come to this place for a reason, and his inability to understand it spiraled through him in ever-widening gyres of anxiety and anger.

"Tell me. . . *Tell* me!" he heard himself saying in a harsh, urgent whisper. The words poured over him in a dim cascade of incomprehension. Maddening and terrifying at the same time.

* * *

"Okay, that was weird. . . ."

Kevin's voice penetrated the darkness like a burst of light, and Cort had the sensation of having been dredged up from a deep anesthesia.

"What? What happened? Jeez, Kevin, that was nuts."

"Tell me about it. I think I'm a believer. I just don't know yet what I'm believing."

Cort checked his watch. An hour had passed since he'd looked at it, since he'd seen the thing that had been his father. An hour in that state of helpless mental paralysis.

"I think we can leave now," said Cort. He twisted on the maglite and pointed its beam towards the door to upstairs hall.

"No argument here." Kevin stood, held the video recorder up like a trophy. "I think I got it all, man."

* * *

An hour later, they were in an all-night diner on the Beckley Turnpike. Kevin proclaimed he was hungry enough to eat a snake out of a boot—whatever that meant—and he broke into a chorus of a

"La Donna Mobile" when he saw the diner through the wind-shield.

He'd wanted to replay the video right after they'd left the Hoetzel house, but Cort had said no. He didn't know why, but he just wasn't ready to see that image again just yet, and honestly, he was afraid of both possibilities of hearing or *not* hearing what his father had been trying to tell him.

Now he sat in a booth at 3:30 in the morning, waiting for Kevin to get back from the restrooms so they could order. Cort stared at his reflection in the black glass of the window, mentally replaying the image of his father looking oddly curled and twisted. There had been something elemental and scary about it, but he had no idea why.

"Hey!" said Kevin as he slapped a thin newspaper down on the Formica tabletop. "Dig this. I saw it up by the front counter."

Looking down at the weekly rag from Beckley, Cort could not avoid the big letters across the top: "Plans to Re-Open Pick-man Bring Hope," said the headline. He picked it up and read the short article, which told of a large energy conglomerate's plan to re-open a series of abandoned coal mines in the area—including the Pickman Mine. Citing advances in technology, a representative of General Energy, said all the targeted mines would yield more coal than thought possible generations earlier. Cort scanned it for any specific mentions of the Pickman disaster or even something *more* specific about his father, but there was nothing.

"So what am I supposed to be digging?" he said.

"C'mon," said Kevin as he pulled a menu from the metal rack at the end of the table. "You know as well as I do—there ain't no such thing as coincidence."

The waitress, a woman who looked exactly like the one you'd expect to be working the graveyard shift of a backwoods diner, approached them.

"Ready?"

Kevin ordered the Number 3 Special Breakfast. Cort just had coffee and toast.

As she shuffled off toward the kitchen, Kevin grabbed the paper, rolled it up and held like a club. "You think there's nothing to this?"

"What, they want to open the mines. So?"

Kevin tilted his head, gave him an expression that said *don't give me that.*

"This is *connected,* man. I don't want to sound crass, but listen, Cort, your father is *buried* in that mine, okay? And now that somebody's gonna open it, they're gonna be opening his grave. Now, c'mon, you *know* that!"

"Okay, and if I did? What're you saying?"

"It's obvious. I mean, didn't you wonder, like, why now? Like, after all this time, why was your father trying to contact you?"

The waitress appeared with mugs of coffee that looked like they'd been part of a civil war mess kit, then slipped away. Cort used the interruption to gather his thoughts. Kevin was, of course, correct. He'd scored to the heart of the question that had been capering at the edges of Cort's conscious thoughts. It made total sense his father would want to contact him for a definite reason. Problem was, Cort wasn't sure he wanted to know what it was.

He looked at Kevin, who was waiting for a real answer.

"Okay, so yeah, of course it occurred to me. But I had no way to figure it out."

"You do now," said Kev, holding up the rolled paper and using it as a pointer to indicate the small video recorder next to his plate. "Soon as we finish the chow, we check this out okay?"

* * *

But it didn't work. . . .

The video was infuriatingly unclear, suggesting more than it displayed, and the sound was a little worse. They listened to the stream of garbled words mixed with an odd static. Someone was speaking, but the words seemed speeded up or slowed down.

It wasn't until they got back to Baltimore, where Kevin focused his manic energies to get some answers. First thing he did was Google the Pickman Mine, where he found a surprising number of articles about the accident. Apparently, an incident over a mile down sparked a panic or a riot. None of the sources described what caused the disturbance, but it was clear something happened to inspire a mass exodus from the mine. There were several explosions, and twenty-three men were trapped in a connector shaft. Rescuers were able to communicate with the miners by cable-phone, but the foreman, a man named Ray Fallon, had told them there was no way to get them out. Another explosion of unknown origin further sealed the main shaft, and that was the end of it. Rumor and speculation had Fallon setting off the explosion that buried everybody for good.

When Kevin shared all this with Cort, he understood what had driven his mother from the town, and he had a feeling he understood why his father might have wanted to tell him he was no villain.

But there was actually more to the story, and it wasn't until Kevin downloaded a bunch of sophisticated audio software that things deepened. Cort sat in Kevin's office filled with fifties movie-monster posters, boxes of collectable baseball cards, and floor-to-ceiling racks of CDs and books; he watched his friend hunched over his keyboard analyzing the digital audio tracks from the video recorder.

"What we have here is called an EVP," he said in his excited old scientist voice. He had a special affection for Cecil Kellaway's interpretation in *The Beast from 20,000 Fathoms.* "Electromagnetic voice phenomenon. I'm going to execute some the enhancements. We can figure out speed, time, timbre, and see if things get more clear."

"How'd you figure this out?"

Kevin looked at him with his *are-you-kidding-me* expression. "E. Kevin Fitzgerald is a cheen-yus! Don't you forget it."

"So exactly how do you do it, Genius?"

"I'm going to slow down the sound, stretch the range, and stuff like that."

"If you say so. . ."

Cort watched and listened as Kevin diddled and moused and clicked. The screen displayed a digital image of the voice-track—an endless moving landscape of jagged peaks and valleys. This went on for a while, then he announced they were ready. Kevin clicked the *play* button on the menu bar, and the little Klipsch speakers at the corners of his desk crackled with sound:

. . . .and none of 'em . . . what really happened down here. . . . Okay with me, all this time . . . okay with me . . . till now . . . Now they

thinkin' about comin' down . . . back down here, son . . . and they can't . . . . you gotta tell 'em . . . they can't . . . they can hate me all they want . . . I'm beyond that now . . . .okay with me . . .

"Can you stop it for a sec?" Cort felt a wave of recognition crash over him. The voice echoed from the distant shore of his childhood. The inflection, the cadence, the way each word was pronounced. So many years ago. . . He had forgotten the sound of his father's voice, and now it came rushing back with a force and an immediacy he hadn't been ready for.

Clicking it off, Kevin looked at him with surprise. "What? What's the matter? You okay?"

Cort explained his unexpected reaction. "I'll be okay. Go on, let it run. I'll be fine."

Kevin nodded, selected *play* again.

*. . . but no **way** they come back here . . . but there was no way . . . . no way to tell 'em back then . . . Ray Fallon wasn't keepin' help from gettin' in . . . I was keepin' the thing from gettin' **out** . . . they come down the main . . . and they mos' likely will . . . they gotta keep connector 14 sealed . . . you tell 'em that . . . and it'll be okay . . . so just know, son. Your daddy loves you . . . loves you still . . .*

Cort had been watching the digital display as he listened to the voice. Suddenly, it flattened out, defining the subsonic hum of the now-silent speakers.

"That's it," said Kevin.

"Yeah. . ."

Neither of them spoke for what felt like a long time. Then they replayed it a couple more times. Each time, it sounded more clear. Cort transcribed some of it, and then they went about the careful analysis that would assure both of them not only had they

31

heard the same thing, but also *understood* the same thing.

Cort had never thought he was an overly emotional person, but he was having trouble with this one. While Kevin had usually been the excitable, unpredictable element, Cort found himself depending on his friend to take the vanguard on whatever they would be doing next. He told him as much.

"Wow, old buddy," said Kevin. "I can't imagine what you're going through. I mean, hearing your dad like this. . . . Gotta be weird."

"Yeah, but you need to get me past that. What'll we do about what he said? What *can* we do?"

* * *

Operating from the premise that it wouldn't be a good idea to re-open the Pickman Mine, Cort let Kevin handle their plan to penetrate the corporate veil with a few important-looking certified letters from their DC law firm pals. They followed that up with phone calls and even a personal visit to General Energy's South Region headquarters.

Through all of it, Cort tried to keep his thoughts centered on a single track—that the mine shouldn't be re-opened, or if that was unstoppable, at least the one part would remain sealed off. Trying to convince anyone within the power cubicles of a juggernaut like General Energy was more than daunting and properly belonged in the territory of the hopeless. But they'd sworn to themselves they would press on and be the squeaky wheels until some grease was thrown their way.

What Cort tried *not* to think too hard on was exactly *what* his father had run into down there in that anthracitic hell. What could have driven the man to his extreme solution?

And Cort had been pretty successful at not thinking about any of it. . . .

Until he realized: a story that begins with a letter should probably end with one.

Until he opened the letter from a General Energy engineer which read, in part:

. . . And I thought you would want to know the company was successful in keeping the connecting tunnel (no. 14) sealed. Suspecting it had become a sarcophagus for the trapped men, we agreed with your wish it remain undisturbed as much as possible.

The only compromise to this decision involved a fiber optic camera snaked into the tunnel for verification purposes only. You were correct, Mr. Fallon—we did indeed encounter human skeletal remains—although one of the bodies appears to be entwined with what appears to be the exoskeleton of a large, unidentifiable creature.

Our engineers submitted the images to pan-academic crypto-paleontological database, and we have received a very interested query from Professor Charles L. Grant of the Miskatonic University. We shall keep you informed.

Trent Walters

THE CHAPMANVILLE DEAD

Trent Walters researched this story through the patented Immersion Method™: He became a ghost himself (You can, too, if you order his special kit for the low price of only $19.95!). His work appeared in *The Golden Age SF anthology, Electric Velocipede, Lady Churchill's Rosebud Wristlet, Pindledyboz,* and *BSFA's Vector.* Forthcoming are works in *Full Unit Hookup, Grendelsong, Triangulation,* and *Visual Journeys.* Also forthcoming is his poetry chapbook, *Learning the Ropes,* from Morpo Press.

At 2 A.M. on the day Chapmanville High began, the alarm under my pillow bleep-bleeped and jerked me wide-awake. I slammed it off, dressed in two pairs of clothes in case I needed a quick change, and slipped my arms through the straps on my backpack with my stupid name stitched across the back: *Cassiopeia.* I headed south on highway 10, kicking stones and shuffling past Sunset Court where I set off backyard dog alarms.

Mom had been on to me about all the missing food recently and about how fat girls don't date. Why I'd date a local boy was beyond me: Rednecksville with their gun racks, pickup trucks, and twangy country music. A few bumpers sported Confederate stickers. Hello? West Virginia was abolitionist, knuckleheads. Truth be told, I loved them in my way—Mom, rednecks, and the nicer knuckleheads even. I only left because I hated dead people. Chapmanville was too fond of the dead. I didn't realize until Daddy left.

When the sky lightened up, I was still in Godby Heights. I'd hoped to be on the other side of Pecks Mill, but the heavy backpack slowed me down. With everybody driving to work, somebody was bound to spot me and call Mom.

Tired, I crossed to the Freewill Baptist Church. Since it was my freewill to run away, they'd respect that. We'd gone there a few times when Daddy first got saved from beer and beer-driven fists— before Daddy ran off with some jailbait field-commander band girl.

The church was unlocked, so I slipped in and tiptoed to a back pew. I peeled open some beef jerky and chewed it over so I'd have energy to finish the journey. Using my backpack as a lumpy pillow, I fell asleep.

* * *

Daddy was stretching his football-sized hands toward my throat— his face and fingers leprous with decay—when I woke with a lump of unfinished jerky in my mouth. I could have choked on it.

Strangely colored light streamed through the stained glass upon a broad-shouldered man standing at my feet. My heart skipped, thinking it was Daddy.

The big man was talking on a cell phone: "Donna Quackenbush? Pastor Bill from Freewill. Anything turn up missing this morning? Something strawberry blonde?"

How'd he know? Then I remembered my name on the backpack. How many kids had such a stupid name? He grabbed my foot and wiggled it. I jerked it away and set it on the floor.

He smiled with annoyingly infinite patience. "She's fine. Just finished her beauty sleep."

* * *

Mom was furious. In her starched waitress uniform, she made

scratchy sounds as we marched to the Trans Am. Who the heck drove Trans Ams? Surely, it reminded her of the jerk who used to beat her. "Get in," she said as if she hoped I'd try to argue.

I slid in and put my backpack on my lap. Mom's hands were shaking so she couldn't fit the key into the ignition. She gave up and looked out the window. "Do you know what it's like working two jobs to put food on the table? Spending nearly fifteen years to raise an ungrateful child? No, or you wouldn't have run away."

She composed herself to put the key into the ignition but, suddenly, slammed her palms on the steering wheel. "What did I ever do? What was so God-awful?"

I was about to tick off a list—people forget how mean they can be—but then I saw me from her red-rimmed eyes. Her daddy left her, her husband, now me. "It's not. . . you. It's Chapmanville. The whole school will know by the time we get back. I won't hear the end of it. Because we have a tiger mascot, the school website plays that corny 'Eye of the Tiger.' The counselor started his egghead 'Character Counts' luncheon-thing to tell us how to be nice. A whopping tenth of the town graduates from college, and a third of the high school drops out. Who can blame them? Our building looks like a farm shed. The state has zero imagination when it comes to naming. A farmer's wife leaves him so they call the town 'Shegon.' Mudfork forks and gets muddy. And"—I'd saved the worst for last—"parents name their daughter after a boring constellation because they'd conceived her under stars."

Mom no longer looked sad. Calm, she started the engine, checked traffic, and pulled out onto Route 10 going north. "I didn't realize I'd raised a shallow daughter."

Trees zipped past the window. "I'm not."

Her voice mimicked: "I don't like the way they name things."

My eyes blinked back their brimming. "You don't know half of what Dad did while you went crying to your Mama."

"What are you talking about?"

She tried to wipe my cheek but I elbowed her arm away. "He made me watch films about dead people slaughtering the living. Said he'd rise from the grave if I ever told what he did to you."

"He what?"

"I don't care if he got religion. I'm glad he ran off with that girl."

"He didn't run off with no girl."

"Okay, he killed her. That's why the ceiling tiles in the band office bleed."

"Cassie, that's rust. From old pipes."

"They use PVC, Mom."

"Your father didn't know the girl. He didn't coach when she was in high school."

"Only because he came to work drunk. That's beside the point. Everywhere you go, Chapmanville's chockfull of dead. Crawley Creek was named after a dead soldier from Tennessee. Ghosts haunt abandoned mines. I can't walk through town without flashing on those movies and Dad's threats."

We pulled into the drive beside our trailer. "You've got to remember the good times when your dad sobered."

I squeezed my eyes. Good times? Even sober, he could barely control his rage. Maybe he didn't smack Mom, but when he chopped wood out back—that axe cracking through logs—you heard whose head he thought about.

37

"Remember the state fair?" Mom asked.

I hazily recalled riding Dad's broad shoulders though I was too old, eating sticky pink cotton candy, and wiping it in Dad's hair, him pretending outrage and acting impotent to harm the girl on his shoulders, crashing into telephone poles as if to knock me off but hurting his head instead. Yeah, he'd been all right—once in his life.

Mom put her hand on my knee. "Skip school. Take a nap. Watch the soaps. But promise to look at the band room with me after school. Together. Whenever you see the ceiling tile, you'll laugh. Okay?"

"I'm not going out for band."

Mom patted my knee. "First, look at the tile. Then decide."

* * *

Mom came home that evening, flung off her apron, and unbuttoned her blouse as she walked to her bedroom.

I flicked off the TV. "Mom?"

"In a hurry," her voice sang from the closet. Clothes plopped on the floor. "Bar called. We need the money. But you're still going to go see the band room ceiling." Mom was fast. She swept in with the same skirt but wore what she called her best-tipping blouse and heels. She checked her makeup in the mirror. "I called Mr. Retz, the counselor."

"You what?"

She touched up her lipstick and glanced at me in the mirror. "He's a friend of the family. He made me explain why you weren't there. Wipe that look off your face. How else would you get in the band room?"

* * *

38

Mr. Retz's windowless office was paneled in faux wood. On the door, a sarcastic poster urged teens who knew everything to move out and get a job. Apparently, the poster was so clever, a third of the school agreed.

Mr. Retz stood and unbuttoned his sports coat to reveal a sport shirt, spectacularly hideous, underneath. He was shorter than Dad but his chest was wider than a beer keg. "Come in!"

I mumbled, "I'm already in."

"Have a seat at my desk. I want you to read something on my computer." His chair did look more comfortable than the hard orange plastic seat he had for students. He kept one hand on the back. "Did you know your father and I were good friends?"

"Whatever." I sat on the edge of his chair, with my hands in my lap, arms tucked in. The computer listed ghost sightings in West Virginian towns. Chapmanville's said a man had been murdered in a swamp where the band room was. I hadn't heard that.

"Notice any patterns?"

"They're all ghosts."

He chuckled. "Besides that." He leaned over—reeking of body spray that was popular among teens—laid one hand on the armrest near my elbow, and tapped the screen with a fingernail. "Here." He paged down and pointed out more.

I leaned away from him. "So a lot are schools. So what?"

"So they're places where people have too much free time. Compare these two. One's an elaborate story while this one just has noises and doors that open on their own. What does that tell you?"

"Nothing."

"Ghost stories evolve. I've tested my hypothesis. I emailed the website with a ghostly reason for the red-stained ceiling tiles, and the next year that was the prevailing story." He put a hand on my back. "Discerning patterns. That's the key to what we'll teach you in high school. Let's visit the band room with that in mind."

* * *

Mr. Retz had trouble with the lock. "Too many people jerk on it while it's locked." He clicked the key back and forth. "You know I introduced your mother and father? Your dad and I were thick as thieves. Local football legends. Quite the lady-killers." The door unlocked.

I stepped back and stared at Mr. Retz.

He laughed. "Figure of speech. Means we had our pick of ladies. Your mother is quite the looker, and you're a sight for sore eyes yourself. In the blood." His arm snaked around my shoulders and escorted me in. A dim light shone in back. He took his arm off my shoulders. "Never can find that light switch."

Something swung from the ceiling. An arm. Dripping blood.

"There it is."

The lights came on, and the arm vanished. Or wasn't there.

Mr. Retz fiddled with the door. "Don't want the door slamming so we think a ghost did it. The office?" He motioned toward where the arm had hung.

"You lead."

He entered the semi-dark office. "See? Nothing. Where's that light?" My father's hulking shadow stepped from behind the office door brandishing a music stand. He swung at Mr. Retz. A scream stuck in my throat.

Fluorescent lights flickered on. The music stand clattered to the floor.

"Must have knocked that over. Look." He pointed up and smiled. "Clean white ceiling tiles."

A small red dot seeped through the tile. A drop fell and splattered music sheets on the desk. Mr. Retz put out his hand. "What the. . . ?" A drop fell into his hand. He looked up at the red oozing across the tiles.

"You." I backed away. "You killed that girl, the field-commander." I ran for the door.

"Cassie!"

I slammed into the steel door and jerked violently at the handle. It was locked.

He leaned calmly against the office door. "Cassie, I wouldn't harm a hair on such a beauty. Ask her yourself. I'll take you to her. She's fun. She likes the girls I bring over."

"If she's alive, why do her parents think she ran away?"

His face grew dark. "Because her parents were religious prudes like your father became."

"Then. . . you killed. . . my father. . . and stuffed him up there."

His smile didn't put her at her ease. "Why would I hurt my best friend?"

"He promised to turn you in. You'd go to jail. You'd never set foot near a school again. Anywhere you moved, neighbors would learn your past and shoot you dirty looks whenever you stepped out your door."

He sauntered across the room. "How could anyone get away with murder in a small town?"

"Don't come closer."

He spread his hands toward the empty room. "Or you'll

41

what, scream? The room is soundproofed for a high school band. I lift weights. I wrestled at state. There isn't a man left in town who could take me."

I knew one. I turned off the lights.

Kealan Patrick Burke

HOW THE NIGHT RECEIVES THEM

Kealan Patrick Burke is the Bram Stoker Award-winning author of *Currency of Souls, The Turtle Boy, The Hides, Vessels, Midlisters, Ravenous Ghosts,* and *The Number 121 to Pennsylvania,* and the editor of the anthologies: *Taverns of the Dead, Night Visions 12, Brimstone Turnpike, Quietly Now,* and *Tales from the Gorezone.* He lives in Ohio with his wife, son, two mad cats, and a sneaky ghost who likes to applaud for no good reason.

It is not how you walk, or where, or how far. It is all in the sound of the steps and how the night receives them.

Carrie shakes her head and her hood chafes her cheek. She hates the coat almost as much as she hates the woman who forced her to wear it, but secretly she is glad of its warmth, no matter how heavy and uncomfortable it feels around her thin frame. A sigh sends a cloud rolling out to join the fog. The skin across her face feels tight, like new leather; her eyes water. Her lips are cracked dry and raw.

It is not how you walk. . .

The dense fog turns the night to silver as it smothers the moon and steals its light. The vaporous clouds are like damp kisses against her face.

The words the man said made no sense to her, and she wishes she could stop thinking about them. But every time she tries to focus on something else—like her mother's worsening habit—

those words come again, speaking over unrelated images like a displaced narrator.

It's a quote, the detective, who she has come to call The Poet, told her when she'd queried their origin, *from the one and only poem I ever wrote.*

It's beautiful, she'd replied, though she wasn't sure that was true. She'd wanted to ask what the words meant, but refrained from doing so for fear the man with the sad green eyes and hangdog face would consider it rude. All she knew for certain was that the words, whatever the meaning behind them, clearly had greater significance to him than they would ever have for her. *You should write more of them. Seems like you know how.*

He'd smiled then, his car moving alongside her, the window down, the lights picking up the first gathering wisps of fog. *Sometimes there's enough darkness in the world without adding to it under the guise of something pretty,* he'd said, and she hadn't understood that either. So she'd shrugged, dug her hands into the pockets of her heavy red coat and stared down at her feet.

I think if you have that kind of a talent, it'd be a shame not to use it, she told him.

The Poet had nodded, eyes distant. *All my talent, if that's what you'd call it, goes only one way these days. Into the worst kind of darkness. And no one ever tries to make something pretty out of it, because there's nothing pretty to be had. Just . . . darkness.*

But you help people, don't you? Your job is to be a voice for those who can't speak for themselves.

He'd smiled at her again, the warmest smile she'd ever seen from him, and nodded. *That's very profound. And true, I guess, though it doesn't always feel like it. Some of the time it feels as if we're just here to* bear witness to the acts of monsters. To validate their efforts by seeing what they've done.

He'd fallen silent, as he often did. She had less than a mile to walk, less than a mile in his company, but the silence as he accompanied her was so much better than the quiet when she was alone. The rustling of nocturnal animals in the brush between the trees, the grating shriek of possums, the sharp bark of raccoons, the clamor of deer as they fled at the scent of her, the imagined sound of footsteps lost in the echo of her own . . . none of these things seemed threatening when he was by her side.

Tonight, however, as she reflects on all he said the night before, she is alone.

The fog is thicker.

The silence, deeper.

It is all in the sound of the steps...

The cold tries to infiltrate her coat, tries to creep up her sleeves and down the open throat. She folds her arms and hugs herself tight. Drops from an earlier rain plop to unseen puddles on the road. Leaves fall wetly to the asphalt.

Half a mile to go . . .

Though there are no landmarks visible by which she might gauge her progress, she knows where she is. Every night for the past six months she has walked this road and the feel of it beneath her feet has become familiar.

A slight rise here as she passes the turnoff to the Lincoln Travel Center.

A rough, fissured patch there where half-hearted attempts have been made to repair holes in the road.

The sign telling her where she is: *Route 50*.

The hill, lost in clouds of gray-white, the graveyard some-where beyond the phalanx of warped ancient trees to the right, hidden from view so travelers have no reminder that death sees this road and visits often.

She shudders at the thought of those silent plots, those vaguely human-sized mounds in the lush grass, those endless rows of chiseled names, all lost in the fog, but most definitely there, for they have nowhere else to be, and no place else will have them.

Behind her, lights blossom in the gloom. She looks over her shoulder, but maintains her pace. She could not have slowed even if she'd wanted to. The distant sound of tires sizzling through puddles. The drone of an engine. She almost smiles, feels a small flutter of excitement in her belly as the car approaches, the lights bullying through the fog to find her. A faint squeak of brakes and the sense of weight pushing along beside her, the whirr of a window being rolled down. Then a voice. Her smile fades, the flutter dies. It is not The Poet, the detective, her friend. It is no one she knows.

"Hey there." A man's voice. Cheery, laced with concern. "Hey Miss, is everything all right?"

She ignores the voice and knows she's being rude, but can't help herself. She doesn't want to acknowledge the man because then he will talk and ask questions for which she has no answers. He will assume the role of guardian, and it does not belong to him. So she walks, and bows her head, her hood hiding her face.

"Miss? Were you in an accident?"

She shakes her head. Maybe if he thinks she's okay, he'll leave her alone.

"Do you need a ride?"

Again, she shakes her head, and strains her ears, hoping to

hear another car on the road. But there's nothing. The thought that he might not come tonight saddens her, so she quickly dismisses it. He will come. He always does. He'll come to see her home.

But she is running out of road, and the man she doesn't know is still watching her, his car keeping pace with her, his concern tangible and vaguely irritating.

"Miss?"

At last she looks his way. The darkness inside her hood shields her for the briefest of moments.

"I can give you a ride if you like."

Then the moon penetrates the protective veil of dark inside her hood and the man's breath sounds like air escaping a punctured tire. He doesn't say anything more. Doesn't even pause to roll his window up. He just jerks back in his seat, hits the gas and the car roars away, spraying water and skidding on leaves, and then there is nothing but red eyes blazing in the dark. Suffused and muted, and gone.

The night grows colder, the fog so thick now that there is nothing to see but white. But she knows the road, knows the feel of it so well.

Sometime later, another car, and now she is nearing home. The road turns sharply to the left and she has almost rounded the bend when she hears an engine growling. A song, faint, turned low, and a window slides down with a hum. Then he is there, and she allows herself a small smile.

"I was wondering when you'd come," she says softly.

For a moment, The Poet says nothing.

She risks a glance around the edges of her hood.

He looks almost ghoulish, bathed by the green glow of the

dashboard lights. His face is sunken, his eyes dirty coins above bags heavy with regret. His thinning hair is unkempt, uncombed. The hand on the steering wheel is like a denuded tree branch, the thin fingers tightening, making the rubber squeak. He does not look at her as he speaks:

"'It is not how you walk, or where, or how far. It is all in the sound of the steps and how the night receives them.'"

She frowns, looks away and concentrates on the road. "Did you write that for me?" she asks.

"I didn't mean to let you down," he says, ignoring the question. "I promised I'd keep you safe."

"I know," she says.

"I couldn't."

"Did you write the poem for me?"

"We found them, Carrie. We found them all. He'd taken the . . . faces, but before he died he . . . told us where to find them."

"I don't want to talk about that."

"He made some kind of perverse mural."

"Please . . . don't."

He shakes his head. A sob escapes him. "'The Surgeon of Salem', they're calling him. He'll be remembered, you can be sure of that, but you, and the others? Only we'll remember you, and that isn't right. He'll be remembered by virtue of his sins. The innocent don't even have their fa—"

Sobs wrack him; he struggles to compose himself.

Alarmed, she glances at him, then away as his eyes turn in her direction.

"When they bury you," he says quietly. "They'll bury you as you were in life, not as he left you in death. It's something, I guess."

"Tell me about the poem. Tell me what it means."

Another car swishes by, but it is traveling in the opposite direction, back where there is nothing but memory. Carrie sees the pale smudge of a woman's face studying them before carrying on.

"He wanted your beauty. Your identity. He wanted to take it from you. To own it." He dries his eyes on his sleeve, talks in a strained voice. "Why? For God's sake, why . . . ?"

Ahead, hazy rectangular lights shimmer in the murk.

Almost home.

"I'll drive this road every night until I can't do it anymore."

She smiles. "I'd like that."

"I see you, you know," he says wistfully. "Just as you were on that last night, and I will always see you that way. You were the bravest, most stubborn girl I'd ever met. Maybe I should have tried harder to convince you not to walk alone."

She clucks her tongue. "But I'm not alone. I have you."

He stops the car and kills the radio. The night becomes a held breath, caught in the throat of fog.

With a shaky sigh, he leans forward, places both hands on the top of the steering wheel, then presses his chin against them.

The girl stops, too. The amber lights ahead beckon.

She turns and steps close to the car, puts her pale fingers on the door and faces The Poet.

"Will you tell me what those words mean? What your poem means? Did you write it for me?"

"You're safe now," he replies. "No one will hurt you again."

She stands there, smiling, watching the man who will never be frightened by the running darkness that fills her red hood, and she leans forward and kisses him softly on his cheek. He doesn't move, but his breath slows and he turns, looks directly at her.

"I can't see you anymore," he whispers, the tears in his eyes trapping green light.

"It's okay. I'm almost home," she tells him, and thinks of her mother, whom she suspects will be drunk, and high, and not at all happy to see her.

"I think I might love you," she says as she gives the man a shy finger wave and moves away from his car, leaving him awash in the verdant glow until the fog erases him and everything else. Then she listens carefully to the sound of her footsteps, to how the night receives them, and hears nothing at all.

Michael M. Hughes

THE BLACKWATER LIGHTS

Michael M. Hughes can't stay away from West Virginia. He went to college in Elkins and spends many weekends in Great Cacapon and Berkeley Springs. He has crawled through West Virginia's caves, hiked its woods, climbed its mountains, and swum in its rivers. He's convinced West Virginia is not only one of the most beautiful places in the U.S, but one of the spookiest. He lives in Baltimore with his wife and daughter, where he writes fiction, lectures on paranormal topics, and performs as a mentalist.

I've covered some crazy stories in my time at the *Morgantown Weekly*. The guy in Charleston who cooked his mother's Shitzu and fed it to his kids. The snake-handler church in Camp Creek. The miner in Braxton County whose gray matter turned to Swiss cheese because he ate too many fried squirrel brains. The ginseng prospector "gang wars" of Kanawha County—that one got me first place in the feature story category from the Association of Alternative Newsweeklies. A Pulitzer it ain't, but hey, it's something.

I was the go-to guy for the weird stuff. So when my editor asked me to cover a bunch of UFO enthusiasts ("flying saucer whack jobs" was his term), I packed up, made a reservation in the only hotel in Blackwater—the Blackwater Inn, natch—and hit the road. I didn't expect to get a good story out of it. The guy I'd spoken to on the phone, Baker Grayson, had seemed hesitant to speak to me. He'd written a book on mysterious phenomena, with a chapter about something called the Blackwater Lights—mysterious balls of orange light that appeared regularly over the town. I didn't have time to read the book before I left, but he promised to give me a copy when I met him.

Baker eyed me up suspiciously when I introduced myself. He was in his sixties or seventies, grizzled and shifty eyed. He wore dark blue polyester pants and a matching, dandruff-dusted jacket, and smelled like fried food and cigarettes. He probably thought I was a government agent sent to infiltrate his group, but I managed to convince him of my bona fides by using every reporter's favorite trick—a trip to the bar. A couple of beers and shots of whiskey later, I couldn't get him to shut up.

"The history of the lights goes back thousands of years," he said.

"You don't say?" I pretended to scribble in my notebook.

Baker lit a cigarette. "Blackwater was built on top of Indian mounds, you know. The entire town is basically sitting atop a complex of mounds, built by the Adena—the mound builder culture—long before the white men came. They built the mounds because of the lights. The area has always been a place of power. And a gateway to other worlds."

I nodded. The usual new age claptrap, always with an Indian connection to give it legitimacy. "So the aliens are drawn to Blackwater—because of this power thing—and they fly through the gateway?"

He shook his head and sighed. "No. That's not it at all. This has nothing to do with aliens."

"What do you mean? When I spoke to you on the phone, you said you ran a UFO study group. Didn't you say that?" I held up the copy of his self-published book, *Mysteries and Monsters of*

West Virginia, and pointed to the colored-pencil cover art depicting a standard-issue, multicolored flying saucer hovering over a mountain. "This looks like a spaceship to me."

He glanced around the bar. Once satisfied that we weren't being overheard, he lowered his voice. "Look, the cover is meant to sell books. My wife's cousin drew that. But the Lights have nothing to do with aliens from other planets. They're not from outer space— they're from *inner* space. Other dimensions. Other realities."

I sipped my Pabst. "Okay, I can buy that. But how are you sure? From what you've told me, people see lights in the sky. Most people think of aliens when they see that kind of thing. Right?"

"Most people are stupid." He stared at me, snorting. "They have no idea what's going on. They see something strange in the sky, so they assume it's a spaceship because that's what they're taught to believe. That's what the government and the media *want* us to believe. But those of us who have not just seen the Lights, but *interacted* with them—we know better."

Now it was getting interesting. I ordered another round. Finally a possible angle—I might be able to pull a story out of this after all. "Can you explain what you mean by interacting with them?"

He smiled. "Maybe tomorrow night at our meeting. You should talk to Crawford. He has the answers. He's the one who helped me understand what's going on."

I wrote the name in my notebook. *Crawford.*

Baker drained his whiskey. "We're meeting in the woods. You'll have to park at the end of a dirt road. We'll have a little bit to eat, then take a trail to Five Rocks."

"Five Rocks?"

"An old monument, like Stonehenge." He pulled out his wallet, but I shook my head.

"I can write this off. Give me directions."

I slept uneasily that night. I wasn't sure why, but the name Crawford kept echoing in my head, buzzing around like a wasp.

* * *

The drive took longer than I'd expected. My Honda Civic bounced and shimmied along the dirt track that vaguely resembled a road. I smoked cigarettes, sipped from my flask, and turned up *The Who's Greatest Hits* to drown out the incessant drone of crickets and bullfrogs. My windshield was thick with bugs, smeared in yellowish arcs by my wipers, and my odometer was broken, so I had no idea how far I'd come or how far I had to go.

Finally—light. I pulled up next to a group of vehicles. People milled about around a Coleman lantern sitting in the bed of a truck, their faces washed in its bluish glow. Baker greeted me with a stiff handshake. "Thought you weren't going to make it."

"Me neither. That road is something else."

He smiled. His eyes were wide, his face twitchy, like he'd drank three pots of coffee. "We're getting ready to head out to the rocks. Have a cup of punch. And some pâté." He pointed to a punch bowl and a plastic container.

"Nah, I'm all right." *Pâté?*

"Please. Lily made it. Wild mushroom. It's a long hike to the rocks—you'll need some fuel. Trust me. It's good."

I poured a tiny cup of the punch and downed it. I scooped some of the pâté onto a cracker. It was earthy and strong, like porcinis or morels. But the aftertaste was odd. I poured another cup of punch to chase it away.

"Not bad," I lied. "So what are we doing? Why are we meeting in the woods?"

Baker touched my shoulder. "It's just what we do."

I nodded. "Okay. Are we going to look for the Lights? Is this like a . . . light-spotting party?"

A tall, thin man walked out of the darkness and stood next to Baker.

Baker looked up, then turned to me. "Ben, I'd like to introduce you to Crawford."

Crawford's eyes startled me. They were large—abnormally so. And potent. I'd seen eyes like that only once before, when I interviewed a leader of a tri-state meth gang in the state pen—orbs as cold and merciless as a rattlesnake's. And *intelligent*. His skin was pale almost to the point of translucence, and his gray hair hung loosely over his shoulders. He extended his hand. His pinky nail was long and curved. A cokehead?

I shook his hand. Cold and damp, but strong.

"You're the reporter from the *Weekly*?"

"Yes. Ben Smith."

Baker and Crawford just stood there, smiling. I reached into my back pocket and pulled out my notebook. "Crawford . . . is that your first name or last name?"

Crawford raised his finger to his lips. "We'll talk later. We don't have much time."

He turned and walked away. Some story I'd have when this was over—*How I Wasted My Night Sitting in the Dark with a Bunch of Pâté-eating, Punch-swilling UFO Nuts.*

Crawford led the way along a thin, rocky trail. Baker walked in front me, while an attractive, red-haired woman followed me. There must have been twelve or thirteen of us, marching along like Scouts, winding our way deeper into the woods.

"Ouch." I stumbled on a root. Baker caught me. I smelled his breath, hot and swampy and scented with the hideous mushroom pâté. "My balance is a little off," I said. It might have been the darkness and the unfamiliar surroundings, but the simple act of walking had gotten very complicated.

"Careful there. It's going to get a little rough when we go up the hill to the rocks. Grab onto me if you need to, or Lily will help you."

Any other time I would have relished the touch of a woman's hand—especially one as good looking as the woman following me. But I didn't want to touch these people. Something about the whole lot of them was unnerving me. I'd been in some rough situations on my beat, and this one seemed rather tame on the surface. But my paranoia ratcheted up with every step I took deeper into the forest. I'd stopped smoking pot years before because of paranoia, and at that moment it felt like I'd powered through a joint of potent skunk. They kept smiling at each other, as if they were all in on a joke.

Keep it together, Ben.

We marched on. I had lost sense of time, but it seemed like an hour of nonstop hiking. A hill loomed ahead, rising out of a clearing like the dome of a moonlit skull. Red curlicues, like phosphorescent vines, moved in my peripheral vision. Amazing how darkness can play tricks on one's eyes. I wobbled, and grabbed onto the back of Baker's jacket.

He turned, that stupid, knowing smile on his face. And then

his face blurred and smudged, as if he was an oil painting and an invisible thumb had smeared his grinning countenance across the sky.

What in God's name?

The earth swayed below me. Something was very wrong. Lily grasped my shoulders from behind, holding me still.

Barker's face *rippled.*

"What's going on?" I asked. "What did you do to me?" Lily squeezed my shoulders, but I pulled away. Baker stopped smiling.

"Ben, it's okay."

"It's not okay. You drugged me." The Moon hung directly above us—so bright it hurt. I was spiraling into panic, losing touch. *Hold on,* I told myself. *Keep yourself together and you can get out of this. You will get out of this.*

"We didn't drug you, Ben. We gave you medicine to allow your eyes to fully open, to cleanse your perception. So you can see. So you can *apprehend* the totality of the manifestation."

Crawford's oyster-gray face appeared over Baker's shoulder. His eyes widened, pupils nearly blotting out the irises. "Bring him to the circle," he said. "It's almost time."

Baker and Lily led me forward, up the hill. I could barely walk, much less resist. As we neared the summit, the rocks came into view—a circle of five long, jagged boulders. A hand of stone reaching for the Moon. And in the center, a dark, smooth slab. Baker whispered in my ear.

When you see it, Ben, you will understand why It called you here.

The group formed a circle inside the rocks, Baker and Lily holding me upright. I could vomit. Crawford stripped naked and stood on the central slab, arms raised, muscles taut. Everyone stood, quietly, expectantly. The drone of the forest's insects intensified into a roaring buzz, as if a conductor had suddenly motioned for *fortis-sississisimo.*

And then it happened.

Everyone looked up. The group intoned a sound—a deep, resonant *oooooooooo.*

Four stars—*at least, they looked like stars*—brightened simultaneously, flaring and pulsing. They moved, from opposite parts of the sky, and merged into one glowing, orange sphere directly above our heads.

And then it descended.

The group's chant rose in pitch, and Crawford opened his mouth. I've never heard anything like the sound that came out of his lungs, vastly inhuman, insectoid and utterly alien. It was like the buzz of a cicada through a powerful amplifier. The air itself vibrated visibly as his bizarre call grew louder and more insistent.

This is not happening. Not happening.

As the light approached, my legs gave way. No one noticed. I lay on my back, legs twisted, arms splayed above my head. The light stopped. It was enormous, hovering above us, pulsing so brightly my eyes watered. And then something came out of the bottom of it, a black speck against the terrible brightness.

The chorus changed again, this time to an earsplitting *eeeeeeeeeeee.*

What I saw I will never forget, though I wish to God I could. It's etched deeply in the folds of my being, the sheer madness of it burned forever into my cellular memory.

It was very much like a shrimp.

If a shrimp had a mass of phosphorescent anemones growing out of its head. And two long, insectoid forelegs, jointed like a mantis and covered in wriggling cilia. Opaque tubes extruding into wings webbed with a veiny, bat-like membrane. I couldn't stop staring, even as my brain melted down into a puddle of raw fear and lunacy.

And then it began to rain. Warm, gloopy, greasy rain.

That snapped me out of my stupor. I crawled out of the circle, screaming gibberish. Baker stared up at the creature, tears streaming down his face. Crawford stood, arms outstretched as the liquid fell on him, his hideous, inhuman drone melding with the thing's own buzzing cry. I scrambled to my feet. I ran, smacked into a tree, screamed again, got up. The liquid on my skin smelled like scrambled eggs, rotten fish, and bleach. I threw up as I ran, gagging and heaving, and fell face-first into a ditch.

Eventually I made it to a road, and shortly thereafter, got picked up by a Randolph County sheriff when he found me naked and screaming and clawing madly at my face in the middle of Route 33.

* * *

My editor bailed me out. But I didn't work for a long time and never went back to the *Weekly*. I rarely left my home, and never at night, and eventually collected disability. I developed multiple phobias that still cripple me—spiders, crustaceans, mushrooms, sea life of all kinds, especially supermarket seafood displays. And worst of all—the night sky. I loathe the stars.

On top of that, I was plagued by bizarre synchronicities, poltergeist phenomena, and a white van with blacked-out windows parked outside my apartment for almost two weeks. One morning I woke up five miles from my house, on the top of a hill, with no memory of how I got there—soaking wet and naked.

Most of the weirdness stopped when I moved to Baltimore. Now I work for a rinky-dink community paper in the exurbs, writing about Little League games, PTA meetings, and the intricacies of zoning law. I guess I appear pretty normal to most people. The antidepressant, antipsychotic, and benzodiazepine cocktail bathing my synapses keeps me in a dull, but safe, little cocoon. I work, I go home, I listen to old jazz records, play around on my computer, sleep. Except for the panic attack at the office party, when someone walked by with a platter of pale shrimp and cocktail sauce, I've managed to keep it together. In public, at least.

But every once in a while I wake up, in the dark, my eyes full of tears, and I feel and hear the hum vibrating in my throat, buzzing and droning, so lonely, sad, and lost.

Scott Nicholson

SILVER RUN

Scott Nicholson is the author of six Appalachian Gothic thrillers, including *They Hunger* and *The Farm*. He often bases his work on local folk legends and mountain mythology. He's also published over 50 stories in national and foreign publications, and was a 1999 winner of the Writers of the Future award and a finalist for the Bram Stoker Award. As a journalist in the Blue Ridge Mountains of North Carolina, he has won several state press association awards and has written a number of writing articles. Currently vice-president of the Horror Writers Association, Nicholson plays guitar, raises goats, and tends an organic garden.

Silver Run #19 ain't much in the daytime. A little longer than a football field, it's about three miles from Cairo, West Virginia. Now, I don't rightly know what a "football field" is, but that's what I hear folks say when they lead tours through the tunnel. Walking tours, as if the rail's not good enough for them. O' course, they went and took up the rails some years back, hear they made this into some sort of state park. No appreciation for the Iron Horse, these modern folk.

I don't get out much, so I don't know the ways of the world, and I ain't got a lick of sense for time. Some days it seems I just opened my eyes after the train snipped me in half, when I looked toward the east mouth of the tunnel and saw a couple bits of myself being drug off by the undercarriage of the caboose, dribbling red everywhere. Other days it seems like I been here since the world was born, before these Appalachian hills rose up from the belly of the Earth and then settled down to the long, slow business of erosion. But maybe all days are the same anyway, when you get down to it.

I used to think so. And then she came along.

Pretty little thing, dressed up in her evening gown. You can see right though it, and if I wasn't old enough to nearly be her grandpap, I'd probably look more often. But you can see right through her as well, so I reckon there's nothing ungentlemanly in letting my eyes linger now and then. Even dead, a man's still a man.

She happened during one of the wars, I reckon. The wars all got mixed up for me, because all I remember is the real one, when the Yanks and Rebs went at it and Virginia got split up by Lincoln. I stayed out of that one, I was out in Missouri territory at the time, where the rail was just starting to catch on and Chinamen and Irish were dying by the dozens laying steel and spiking ties. I came back when the B & O line was booming, working the firebox and generally trying not to get tied down with women, card debts, and such, because I figured on heading to the Pacific Coast eventually. And I stayed clear of the women just fine until this latest one.

Well, I didn't really choose her like you might do a wife. And her gown ain't rightly a wedding dress, neither. For one thing, it's not white. It's sort of green like the leaves of a chestnut tree in April. At least when it has color. In the tunnel, color comes and goes, at least to folks like me and her.

That's a little peculiar, but you get used to it after awhile. And—

Tarnation. Here she comes now, so I reckon I'd best see what she wants.

"Have you seen my head?" she asks.

It's in ghost words, 'cause her lips don't move but her voice is in my ears. Maybe that's why normal folk, them still alive, never hear us when they walk through the tunnel. Some of them shiver and hoof it just a little faster, some look around at the slick masonry walls like they expect some secret message to be wrote in the slime.

"I done told you a thousand times, your head's on top of your shoulders where it belongs." She has a fine set of shoulders, smooth as rounded marble and the color of cream skimmed right off the top of the butter churn. Her head ain't no less a marvel, with her hair swooped up in a fancy bundle that only ladies in companion houses wore back in my day. During her time, though, it might have passed for normal ladylike dress-up.

She reaches up to touch her hair, and I can't really tell where her fingers end and the curly locks begin. Still, it's fetching as all get out. "I can't do a thing with it," she says.

I nod. I know my part so well that I don't really have to think it through. I'm like a stage actor or maybe the bass in a barbershop quartet, just delivering lines the way I ought. "You look just fine," I say, though the motion makes me lick my lips. Darned dry lips, what they wouldn't give for a touch of barrel-mash whiskey.

"They'll be coming soon," she says.

"They always do."

You'd think after all these years I'd know how to dress for the occasion. I never had a worry over it before she came along. I'd just hoof it around in my old wool pants and cotton shirt. The holes in my clothes never troubled me none, because there wasn't much difference between the hole and what it was supposed to be covering up. But I wouldn't know where to find clothes even if I wanted them.

There in the early days, before I settled down to this notion of just what *forever* means, I'd go off half-cocked. More rightly, I'd either be floating around three feet off the ground, trailing some see-through innards where my belly got sawed in half by a set of steel wheels, or else my legs would be walking around with nothing to guide them. Not that they got much guidance even back when my brains was attached, considering I spent most of my breathing life balanced in the cab, shoveling like I was feeding the devil.

"What do you suppose it's like out there?" she says.

She's looking out the mouth of the tunnel, down to the north fork of the Hughes River. A soft fog rises from the water, seeping into the gold-and-red forest. Beyond the trees, a collection of lights are winking on, one after another, like dead fireflies pinned against the horizon. Over time, the number of lights have doubled and tripled, and I reckon that's as good a way to mark the years as any, because the stars have pretty much stayed the same. Back in my day, Cairo was the glass marble capital of the world, and sometimes I think those marbles are not toys but eyes, looking back from the forgotten past like a mirror.

"Same as always," I say, as if I possess the wisdom granted by age. If there's one thing I've learned, but try not to dwell on, it's that foolishness never dies. Otherwise, I'd be in one piece and rotting away quiet in a pine box somewhere.

"Do you think they'll like me?" She touches her hair again.

You can see how this dance has played out over the years. She's lost her confidence, and that's an awful thing in a woman. Sure, I'm a little beyond gentlemanly judgment, and my coarser nature somehow uncoupled when the boxcars between my skull and my legs jumped the tracks, but darn it, a man's still a man. "You'll be the belle of the ball," I say.

I reach for my pocket watch. The chain got crushed in the accident, and the watch is stuck on seven minutes before twelve, and I can never figure if that's noon or midnight. Either way, I reckon I'll never reach it, so it don't matter which.

"Almost time?" she asks. She asks a lot of questions. That's women for you. You can lop off their heads and still they keep yakking.

"Pretty soon now," I say, which is as safe a bet as any.

And it probably will be soon. The sun still rises and falls regular, just like it did when I was in one piece, and right now it's settling against the rounded hills, throwing a punkin-colored light across the trees. The horseshoe curve of the tunnel opening, at least on the sundown side, is outlined with light, and out beyond is all the promise of laughter, love, and life. That's probably the worst trick of this condition, knowing there's another way. Maybe there are folks like us out yonder cavorting and cutting up around graveyards and such, just drifting to hell and gone, whichever direction the wind blows. But me and her, all we got is Silver Run and time.

The people usually come from the east end, where it's darkest, but of course, a tunnel runs both ways. I used to think life was just one long rail, running on and on, and all I had to worry about was raking chunks of coal from the tender, pushing the boiler gauge to the red, blinking cinders from my eyes. You don't think much about the end of the line, and when you do, you usually picture it as a nice, easy rolling stop, engine chuffing and wheels creaking as you come up on a comfortable station with lots of friends on the platform to welcome you home. You don't expect to trip over your big toe at full throttle and go end-over-teakettle between the cars.

But a fellow gets used to the notion, by and by. Leastways, I have. Or so I tell myself. What choice do I got?

"Maybe I should change clothes," she says, fretting her head for no reason.

"If you was any prettier, you'd run them off faster than a pack of coyotes in a blood fever," I say. Truth is, she got no other clothes, and if she did change, well, I don't even like to think what might happen if I saw her in her undergarments. Hell, I might even blush, and I don't know what color my cheeks would be. Maybe perdition red or mortuary blue.

"I'll miss you," she says, just like always.

"Comes a time for parting," I say, though it stings a little all the same. Funny how you can just babble out any old words when you're trying to hide what you really feel.

"You've meant a lot to me. We've been through so much together."

Well, that ain't rightly true. We've pretty much been through the same thing once, over and over and over again. But try talking sense to a woman and see where it gets you.

"I never expected somebody like you to come along," I say, which is about as close as I ever brush up against honesty in my current condition.

"Well, you were here first," she says.

And now we come to it. The only real sore point between us. Now, I pretty much nipped any notion of romance in the bud, me being at least a century older than her, but maybe even us dead folk get a little territorial. I don't know how it is with others, since I only got this one example, but I figure if I'm going to be stuck in one place until the end of time, it ought to at least belong to me. But there I go again, acting like I'd expect any different from the female gender.

The ones that come here, they call me The Engineer, though I was always a fireman and never once laid a hand on the throttle. I figure they forgot the way of the steam locomotive same as they forgot every other way except their own, and so it has been since back to the beginning of time. Plus I kind of like the sound: The Engineer. Got more of a ring to it than *fireman* does, like a slow steam whistle on a dewy summer morn.

Trouble is, they don't call me much of anything anymore. They got this new one they come looking for. Fresh kill. "The Jilted Lady," they call her, and darned if that don't got a ring to it, too. I find myself saying it a lot, trying it out on these numb lips. Not that I ever say it aloud, especially to her.

"I have to admit, I had some adjusting to do," I say. "I never expected somebody like you to come into my life."

She doesn't laugh. She's a little humorless, but I chalk it off to the way she got here. Seems I'm always apologizing for the way she is.

"Maybe things could have been different if we'd met at a different time," she says.

Sure as shootin'. I been around long enough to know that it don't matter the reason why it don't work, just that it don't. "You never asked to be here," I say.

Indeed she didn't. She didn't ask nothing, and she couldn't even if she had wanted. That guy wrapped a rag around her mouth tight as a banjo string, and she tried and tried to scream but nary a peep came out. O' course, considering what the guy did to her, I reckon there's a blessing in that, and proof that maybe God is a merciful creature after all.

She wipes at her eyes. Maybe she's crying, or maybe she's fussing with make-up. Looks the same either way. "We were going to be married," she says.

That's plenty enough cause for waterworks, I reckon, and maybe a swift death saved her from a slower, more tortured demise. Then again, her death wasn't all that swift. The fellow who stole her heart took just a mite too much joy in her pain and wasn't in no hurry to end the honeymoon.

The worse part was having to witness the whole thing and not being able to do a thing about it. Try helping someone when you're helpless yourself. Even dead, even ground to government pork beneath the freight cars of B & O's Silver Runner Engine #52, it stings a little.

At least self-pity is a feeling. At least I got that.

"Don't fret over it," I say. "What's done is done."

"I think he'll take me with him tonight," she says, and outside the punkin sky has gone all bruised and purple, rags of clouds sopping up the last daylight.

I check my watch again, wondering for the hundredth time or so why we take our watches and clothes and wounds with us when we cross over. But maybe all we are is scars, the rip we cut in the fabric of the world, and we're lucky to even do that, when you consider how big the universe must be. Like a bucket that spills over from being too full. Maybe me and her is some of the slop.

I want to tell her not to get her hopes up again, but see no reason to be mean. I've had my chances at that, but it ain't my way. She does a good enough job beating herself up the way it is. Instead, I say, "The Good Book says there's a time for every purpose under heaven."

She nods, and her head shifts just a little, and her throat gapes, then a line blacker than shadow creases her neck. Her head falls plumb off, just like it did when her gentleman caller confessed his undying love. It's laying there in the rock bed, jutting between two mossy crossties. She rolls her eyes up at me and smiles the way you do when you're making the best of a bad situation.

"Things happen for a reason," I say. "And things don't happen for the same reason. Or maybe a different reason."

I have no idea what that means. It just sounds like something a wise old coot will say when he's trying to comfort the afflicted.

She stoops down, picks up her head gentle as a kitten, fixes it back in place, then goes through the shenanigans of checking her curls. "I can't do a thing with it," she says.

I gave up praying long ago, figuring providence is best kept to them that have hope, but I'm tempted to offer up a whopper right about now. I figure maybe she's due to move on, maybe she'll catch a caboose one night and just roll on down the line. That ain't the way the legend ought to go, though, because I'm the train fellow. I'm the one they talk about when they walk through here and whisper like they're in church or something.

At least, I used to be. Until The Jilted Lady came along.

"I hear them," she says, giving her hair one more little touch with those slender, pale fingers.

Beyond the tunnel come footsteps, bunches of them, shoe leather kicking up gravel and dead leaves. They usually come in groups, especially at night. More fun that way, I figure. Most times they're giggling, the boys putting on a brave face, the girls acting like they want to be held close and protected. From cradle to grave, and even beyond, females are smart enough to act weak and dumb and vulnerable.

I can't do much about it, since for some reason I'm bound to this little stretch of abandoned rail bed, while The Jilted Lady gets to rove the tunnel from end to end. Best I can do is bite my tongue, hold in my guts, and wait. I'm a right fair hand at waiting.

"Hey," she yells, trying to get their attention.

Lights sweep the tunnel, cast out by what they call *flashlights*, a kind of lantern that burns without fire. Their voices are loud enough to shake the masonry with echoes, but I can't understand a word they say. I like to think they've come looking for The Engineer, but my day is past. Time slides on down the track, spewing sparks from its smoke stack like the vomiting mouth of hell, rolling and rolling on until the conductor's lantern is little more than a wink of starlight against the deep, endless night, and then even that is gone, the rumble fading, the dust settling, and the last whisper of its passing lost in the wind.

"I love you," she says to one of them, and it could be any of them. These days, she's none too choosy. And when you get down to it, I reckon one man's as good as another for a woman's purposes. Don't matter what you're like, as long as you're willing to be owned. Hop whatever boxcar you can when the weather's bad, that's what I always say. Worry about the destination later.

But whichever man she's talking to doesn't hear, or walks faster, or pulls one of the young ladies closer. Their breaths plume from their mouths like the ghosts of locomotive smoke, and none of them mention The Engineer. They hurry on, and by the time they're all the way through the tunnel, it's full dark. Both inside and out.

"He'll be back," she says.

"He'd be crazy not to," I say, adjusting my entrails so I don't look so shabby. "Any man would be lucky to earn your charms."

Sooner or later the eastern mouth of the tunnel is filled with the light of a rising sun and the glory of birdsong.

"Almost time?" she asks.

"Pretty soon now." I check my watch and try not to grin. Things happen for a reason, and they don't happen for the same reason. Or maybe a different one.

She fusses with her hair. The Jilted Lady. I like the way that sounds. I'm only half a man, depending on which end we're speaking of, but I still got my pride. All a woman's got is vanity. There ain't no shame in letting a lady have her way. Not a lot worth fighting over, the way I see it.

Me and her, all we got is Silver Run and time.

And each other, I reckon.

Joseph Nassise

MONEY WELL-EARNED

Joseph Nassise is the author of the internationally best-selling series, *The Templar Chronicles*. He's a Bram Stoker Award and International Horror Guild Award nominee, as well as a former president of the Horror Writers Association. He lives in Arizona with his wife and family.

I make my living killing things.

Sometimes I kill animals. Big ones, usually. Rhinos. Elephants. Stuff like that.

More often than not, though, I kill people.

Somebody knows something they shouldn't know. Somebody sees something they aren't supposed to see. Someone else wants to make certain that they don't talk about it. That kind of thing.

It's not a bad job, as jobs go, and I'm very good at it. One of the best, actually. And that's not my ego talking, either, just a simple statement of fact. The Marine Corps trained me well, way back when, and the years I've spent since as a private contractor have honed those skills even more. I can kill a man at a thousand yards, with the right equipment and time to set up the shot. Believe you me, that's not an easy thing to do.

So I wasn't surprised when I got a message that Big Al Dantoni wanted to see me. I'd done some work for Big Al in the past. He always paid on time and never argued about the price. I like that in a guy. Straight up, ya know?

Big Al was in Vegas, so as soon as I got the message I made

the necessary arrangements and caught the first flight out. Philly to Vegas, with a stop in Phoenix just to be certain I didn't have a tail. I wasn't expecting one, but it never hurt to be cautious. And I'd made a career out of being cautious.

I caught a cab at the airport and twenty-five minutes later, I was being ushered into Big Al's living room. He lived in this big place outside the city, more a compound than a house, really. Word was that Bugsy Siegel himself had built the place back in the thirties, when those guys were throwing cash all over the place like it was going out of style. Back before RICO and federal racketeering statutes and all that.

Big Al was somewhere in the neighborhood of three hundred fifty pounds, but he moved with the grace of a man half his size. He came forward to shake my hand and gestured for me to take a seat.

He wandered over to the bar. "Drink?"

I shook my head. "I'm good."

"Mind if I have one?"

That was Big Al. Always polite. Until you ticked him off and he had some guy like me put a slug through your eye from a few hundred yards out. "Your house," I said with a slight grin. He'd been offering for ten years, and I'd be saying no just as long. It was a familiar ritual. Our way of saying, "Good to see you," or something like that.

Through a variety of cut-outs, Al ran all the construction that took place within the city limits, small and large. If you wanted to build a new hotel or casino complex, or simply wanted to add a room to your house, you went through Al. If you didn't, bad things started happening at your job site. Crew members got hurt. Tools went missing. Product showed up damaged or not at all.

Al poured himself a scotch, a generous one, and wandered back over to take a seat opposite my own.

"I've got a job for you."

That much was obvious, so I kept my mouth shut and waited to hear the rest.

"It's in West Virginia."

I shrugged.

A slight grin crossed his face. He reached down beside his chair, picked up a file, and handed it to me.

It was full of old newspaper clippings, police reports, even a few first-hand accounts written in pen on fading paper. They told an interesting story.

Late in the evening of November 15, 1966, two young couples encountered a strange creature near the abandoned TNT plant outside of Point Pleasant, West Virginia. The creature was described as being shaped like a man, but bigger, in the neighborhood of seven feet tall. It had large red eyes and a pair of monstrous wings that it kept folded against its back. When the couples sped away from the scene, the creature took to the air and followed them right up to the town limits.

Other people saw the creature that night and during the course of the next few weeks. Many of them were reputable individuals, which gave their testimony added credence. The creature, dubbed the Mothman after a villain on the popular Batman television show, was reported as either grey or dark brown and had a tendency to glide when it was aloft. Other strange occurrences were also noted during that time: odd lights in the sky, unexpected problems with televisions and telephones, cars stalled for no reason while passing by the old TNT plant.

The events continued right up until the night of December 15, 1967. On that evening the bridge that crossed the Ohio River outside Point Pleasant abruptly collapsed, killing forty-four people. Some later theories suggested that the Mothman had come to warn the people of the disaster ahead, but that his message hadn't been understood and the people of Point Pleasant, West Virginia, had paid the price.

Whatever the reason, the Mothman wasn't seen again after that fateful night.

I finished reading and tried to collect my thoughts. I was confused and not too embarrassed to say so.

"I'm sorry. I don't understand," I said, looking up.

He smiled. "Your target is right there."

"Who? Someone in these old clippings?" I started leafing through the photocopies again, paying attention to the names, looking for one that made sense given what I knew about Al's business practices.

Then a fat finger entered my frame of vision and came to rest on the picture of the artist's representation of the Mothman. The finger tapped the photo, once, and then Big Al pulled his hand back.

You have got to be kidding me. . . .

I kept my cool. "Let me get this straight. You want me to go to West Virginia. Track down a flying. . ." I glanced down at the paper to get the name right, "Mothman, and bring it back here for you."

He nodded. "Yes, that's exactly right."

In the back of my head I knew that ticking Big Al off was a very bad career move, so I tried to be diplomatic about it. "Al, these articles are more than thirty years old. Since you don't have any newer ones, I'm assuming this Mothman thing hasn't been seen since 1967. The trail is cold, Al, real cold."

His grin got wider, if that was at all possible. He reached down beside his chair and handed me a second file. This one had a couple of recent articles in it from the same paper. They told of lights in the sky and the sighting of a strange figure at night just off Highway 62.

"It's happening all over again," Big Al said. "Which means he's coming back. Except this time it will be different."

He clapped his hands together like a delighted child.

"This time you'll be waiting for him."

He's gone absolutely nuts, I thought to myself. I came within a hairsbreadth of turning him down flat, right then and there, but after a moment I started to think about the financial opportunity in front of me. Al was paying me to go to West Virginia and hunt a mythical creature that hadn't been seen in over thirty years. That meant my daily rate for as long as it took to get the job done, plus expenses. I could probably add in another 10% for hazardous duty pay, too, as there was no way of knowing how dangerous this thing was or what it might be able to do. It was simple math. Added risk equaled a higher price.

I laid it out for him, step by step. How I'd have to observe things for awhile, get the lay of the land. How it would take time to confirm whether the sightings were real or just some country BS. How, if they were the real thing, I would then need to figure out the best way of taking this thing down. I'd have to be thorough and I'd have to be sure; I probably wouldn't get more than one chance to blow it out of the sky.

He listened, nodded a few times, and handed over an envelope stuffed full of cash. "First two weeks pay plus a generous amount for expenses. I'll have a special refrigerator truck on call twenty-four hours a day to pick up the body once you've handled your end of the job."

And just like that, I became the first hit man in the history of violent crime to be hired to kill a myth.

Sometimes this job is just strange.

*   *   *

West Virginia was about what I expected. Lots of trees. Lots of green. Lots of long, lonely stretches of highway. After flying back from Vegas, I'd loaded my Expedition with the equipment I needed and driven south. Interstate 81 took me all the way to I-70 west, which carried me into West Virginia. At that point I switched over to 68, continuing west and crossing half the state before turning south on 79. Another two hours of travel took me into Charleston, where I stopped and had a quick lunch before completing the final leg north into Point Pleasant.

It was a quiet community, perched on the edge of West Virginia with the mighty Ohio River at its back. Population just over 4000. As I drove through the town, scoping things out and getting my bearings, I came to the conclusion that little had changed in the fortysome-odd years since the Mothman's first appearance.

Except for the statue, that is.

It was a large, silver thing, with big wings and red eyes, and was humanoid in appearance. It stood on a pedestal right there in the center of town, with a plaque commemorating that first sighting back in 1966. The statue had been done by a local sculptor, a guy by the name of Bob Roach, and I wondered for a moment if he'd ever seen the thing or if he'd just decided this was what a Mothman should look like.

Probably the latter, I thought to myself.

Turns out the town not only had a statue of their favorite monster, but a museum and an annual festival devoted to him as well. Clearly someone somewhere along the way had the bright idea to capitalize on their notoriety and would probably still be doing so fifty years from now.

That was when I made up my mind.

I knew it was crazy, but I decided then and there to act as if the Mothman was a real target. Big Al was paying me a lot of money and it didn't seem fair to write it all off without checking to see if there was any substance to it.

I needed a place to set up watch. Someplace that was out of the way enough that I wouldn't be noticed by the locals but that had a better than even chance of letting me catch it in the act, if it actually did exist.

The old TNT plant seemed to be my best bet.

The area around the plant comprised several hundred acres of dense woods. Large concrete domes were scattered here and there. The domes had held high explosives during World War II and had fallen into disrepair not too long afterward. A network of tunnels stretched throughout. I imagine it would look something like a giant ant colony, if it could be viewed in a cross-section.

Searching the place was out of the question, and it wasn't because I was worried about encountering the Mothman. There were enough natural dangers to keep me out of a place like that all on its own. Collapsing tunnels, old pitfalls, rats and other vermin.

You needed a team with plenty of rope and a strong GPS signal to do it right, neither of which I had at the moment.

So instead, I set up camp in a thicket on the edge of a slender valley leading to the plant. With a wide area in front and plenty of ground cover to hide in, I would be able to see the Mothman as it was silhouetted against the open sky above. I had my favorite rifle with me, a Remington M24, fitted with a Leupold scope. A memento of my service days. I was confident that if the Mothman put in an appearance, I could shoot it out of the sky with that weapon. Easier than shooting fish in a barrel.

Except the Mothman didn't make an appearance.

At least, not for me. Other folks were seeing him left and right. Soaring across the fields. Standing by the side of the road. Just about everywhere else but the old TNT plant where it had taken up residence the first time around. Every time I went into town I'd hear the latest story, how *so and so had seen such and such* and *what did it all mean?*

Rumors were rampant. What was the Mothman trying to tell them? What disaster was going to befall the community this time? Even the authorities had gotten into the game, with work crews sent out to examine the piling beneath the Silver Bridge, checking for any sign that there might be a repeat of the original disaster.

And still I didn't see a thing.

I vowed that I would spend one more night watching the sky around the old TNT plant and then it was time for a new plan of attack.

It was the first moonless night since I'd arrived. The lights of the town didn't reach this far out and the sky around me was ablaze with stars. I was looking up at them, trying to remember the names of the constellations just to pass the time, when a dark shadow blotted out the stars above me. It was there for just a moment and then it was gone.

But there was no doubt in my mind what I had seen.

I brought my rifle to my shoulder and waited.

It would come back.

I was *sure* of it.

I watched that patch of sky for a full twenty minutes before admitting to myself that I had missed it for the night. I was disappointed, but filled with a strange sense of exultation, too. The darned thing really did exist!

I lowered the rifle and turned around, my thoughts whirling.

The Mothman stood less than a foot away, its wings stretched out above us, its red eyes glowing in the near darkness.

I knew I'd never make it, but I tried anyway.

I swung the rifle up, my finger reaching for the trigger.

The barrel wasn't even halfway to my waist when the Mothman reached out and placed one clawed hand on my shoulder.

An explosion of color and sound filled my head.

* * *

I chose a patch of high ground roughly four hundred yards from where I knew my target would appear. It was far enough away that I could get in and out again without being seen, but close enough that the wind and the natural curvature of the earth wouldn't put too much stress on the shot. I could hit a dime at four hundred yards; I wasn't worried about hitting a target as big as this one from that distance.

I settled in to wait.

It didn't take long.

The target filled the frame of my scope. Thanks to the optics, it looked close enough to touch. I squeezed the slack out of the trigger. Breathed in. Breathed out. Felt my heart beating. Once. Twice. Three times.

In the space between heartbeats, I pulled the trigger.

The gun kicked and roared.

The bullet entered Big Al's head just in front of his ear and exited out the other side in an explosion of blood, brains, and skull fragments. He was dead before his body hit the street.

As chaos broke lose on the street below me, I calmly left position and returned to my vehicle. The half-built parking garage had been a good choice. I'd had an unlimited field of fire and easy access to and from my vehicle. I was six blocks away before the first patrol car even made it to the scene.

Those who claimed the Mothman was a warning of disaster to come were right. I knew it from first-hand experience. I'd seen it all through the Mothman's touch.

The shiny new hotel and casino complex, all eighty-eight stories of it.

The shoddy materials that were used in building the hotel's foundation, because the owners refused to meet Big Al's monetary demands and he intended to teach them a lesson in obedience.

The devastating collapse of the main tower that killed three hundred and twenty-nine individuals, including fifty-seven schoolchildren there for a spelling bee.

With one shot, I kept all that from happening.

Big Al had hired me to kill a monster.

And with the Mothman's help, I'd done that *very* thing.

G. Cameron Fuller

AFTERDAMP

G. Cameron Fuller is a writer-editor with over 25 years experience in all writing phases, from conception through editorial to production. He has written articles for *Writer's Digest* on sudden fiction and a couple for their *Writer's Clinic* column. He is the only person to have won West Virginia Commission on the Arts fellowships in all three literary categories—fiction, nonfiction, and memoir—and lives in South Charleston, West Virginia, with his wife, Karin, and step-daughter, Celeste.

Gravel crunched under the tires as I pulled off the left side of the old Grafton Road, Route 119. I stopped just a few feet before the dozen or so aluminum storage units that constituted the U Stor. The small sheds, barely ten feet high, had the stylized shape of old barns. Peaked roofs, white, with red walls and white sliding doors. I'd never noticed them before, though they looked like they'd been there for years.

A line of cars, already parked on the gravel, stretched in front of the entire line of sheds. Two state police cars, a white van, and a gray SUV with a City of Grafton seal on it. I stepped out, the air already thick in the way of most West Virginia July days, despite it being only midmorning. I patted the side pocket of my shorts to make sure my notebook and pens were there, and looked down into the small valley.

The incline was gentle, the surface covered with grasses and scraggly vegetation. A few trees dotted the slopes, none of them thicker than my body. The unnatural bowl shape and sparse vegetation marked the land as either reclaimed strip mine or sanitary landfill, probably the latter since it sat only a couple miles north of Grafton.

Down below, about 75 yards away at the bottom of the bowl, stood a knot of a half dozen men around a small pit. Three piles of dirt nearby. A uniformed State Trooper with his feet at shoulder width faced the road. He saw me and said something. Two men with nearly identical suits looked up. One of them had a clipboard. I pegged them as detectives, Morgantown most likely. Two men in coveralls had shovels, as did Matt, the man who called me out. He was wearing coveralls over his Trooper uniform. He didn't look up, but stabbed another shovel full of crumbly soil. Another sign this was unnatural land; the natural soil here was full of clay and rocks, much rougher than what flew off Matt's shovel.

I started down with short steps, my body turned sideways for maximum traction. Matt had reached me at home that morning. "Just come on down, Dawson," he'd said, but he wouldn't tell me why. "Should only take a couple of hours. After, we'll get lunch. I'll fill you in."

Matt was the only cold case investigator for the entire state of West Virginia now that Hoppy Estep had retired. The force still hadn't replaced Hoppy, and Matt was working a couple dozen cases. But what was Matt's burden was my boon.

I'd been doing research and leg work for the state and various criminal lawyers for about twenty years, even got my PI license about ten years ago, in 1990, but with Matt's heavy caseload my paid time had more than doubled. I made informal inquiries, interviewed people, and so forth, but my specialty was deep Web research. I circled the edges of the law, mining databases that some people would claim I didn't have legal access to. Other people just said their thanks and paid me for my work. I was thorough and quick.

By the time I'd reached the dig, my legs were covered with bramble scratches and I'd cursed the stupidity that compelled me to wear shorts on the promise of another 90+ day. I'd also recognized Trooper Gooden, an up-and-comer with the Morgantown Dispatch, and the Morgantown detectives Heis and Shade. The other two men were clearly workers with matching City of Grafton hats.

"Oh, you," Heis said, as he saw me. He elbowed Shade.

I walked over to Gooden. "What are we looking for?"

"Morning, Mr. Dawson," he said, extending his hand. He angled his head toward Matt and the hole in the ground, a rectangular trench about three feet deep and five feet long. It reminded me of a grave, and I wondered if Matt was looking for a body. "Sergeant Hall thinks there's something here on that coed case. From 1970."

"Before you were born, Trooper," Heis said. Gooden ignored him.

"This was where they found a pile of the girls' papers and ID back when it was a dump," Gooden said. "Least that's what Sergeant Hall says."

I knew of the case; practically everyone in the state did. Two freshmen, Mared Malarik and Karen Ferrell, picked up hitchhiking on the campus of WVU, their headless bodies found three months later in the woods between here and Morgantown, about eight miles north, just off the Weirton Mine Road. Few people thought the man convicted of the double murder actually did it. He never took police to the bodies, and he never was able to tell them where to find the heads.

"How did you decide. . ." I trailed off, looking around the slopes of land.

"GPS," Gooden said, tapping the GPS unit on his belt. "We triangulated from telephone poles in old police reports." He pointed up to the left side of the row of storage units. "And there." Another pole on the right side, near my car.

For the next hour, those of us watching were pretty much silent, although Heis and Shade began to get restless, trading muttered remarks. The hole deepened. Matt's pace never slowed or paused. A fireplug of a man, he had broad shoulders and gave the impression of extra-long arms and oddly large hands. I took out my notebook and jotted a few words describing the scene, mostly to disguise my discomfort at standing there and not helping while the three of them labored. At last, with the hole nearly as deep as Matt was tall, he stopped. The other two men stopped as well.

"Here," he said, indicating with the point of his shovel. At first I thought it was a large stone, but as he gently scraped away some dirt, I saw what looked like the top of two eye sockets. A human skull.

"Careful now." He set down his shovel, dropped to his knees, and began pushing dirt aside with his hands. "There should be another one nearby."

* * *

I ran my hand over stubble as the first glow of dawn filled my study window. Hitting the Favorites button on my browser to save the URL, I wondered if it was too early to call Matt. The sky was a deepening red, which foretold storms. Least that's what the old rhyme said. There would be a storm in Matt's brain when he heard what I'd found.

Back when Angel was little, this would have been the time of morning Raine would be getting up, getting ready to harangue Monkey into rising and eating her Lucky Charms. But Monkey was in college in Honolulu, and my own lucky charm was more than ten years gone, dead from a blood clot that broke loose from her leg as she slept. All-nighters often left me fatigued and melancholy. Especially on cases like this.

"Something came to my attention last week," Matt had said when we ate in the Grafton diner that afternoon. He'd set down his sandwich and rubbed his hand across his jaw. I'd come to know that as a sign he was trying to arrange things in his mind. Get things straight. Times like this, Matt's every move carried a deliberate weight.

"I know now who really killed Mared and Karen. Obvious back in 1970, '71." He spoke around a huge bite of sandwich. "But no follow-up. Almost a year after the girls were killed, December of 1970, a man was arrested and convicted of murdering an H. L. Cobun in Pendleton County. Cobun's head had been cut off, like you'd dress a deer. Our man had a hunting camp down there and Route 33 runs right from Pendleton to the old Grafton Road here. They found Cobun's head buried eight miles away."

"That's how you knew where to look for the heads." I nosed a fry through the swamp of ketchup, and Matt shrugged. "The dump's eight miles south of where they found the girls' bodies."

"A hunch. I read back through the case file." His gray eyes fixed me, not so much studied as *pinned*. "Those IDs and things were placed in that dump. As if to mark a spot. They weren't just tossed."

"What's the guy's name?"

"Hacker. William Bernard." Matt polished off his sandwich. "Hacker'd already served time for double murder. A couple, both shot in the head in a bar in Fairmont. 1952. He was pardoned in 1966. His wife disappeared in Monongah in 1937. That's what told me. Someone who does that kind of thing—what happened to those girls—doesn't kill just once."

"1937? How old was this guy?"

"Born in 1896. Grew up in Monongah. Coal miner, a hard man. Last records I saw indicated he had black lung, lung cancer. Renal failure. Think he died in prison. You're going to find out everything you can about this guy."

"CIB should be able to give you a thorough background check."

Dwight waved me away. "Don't need to know what he did, just what he might have done. This guy liked killing. I want to know what made him that way."

So I went straight home after the late lunch and began searching. Right away I found newspaper articles written after his conviction for the murder of Cobun. Authorities at the time thought there might be a connection to the coed case. Hacker had coyly said he'd talk only to a reporter who'd written some articles about him.

"I've got something to tell about them girls," he had been reported as saying. "You all ain't gonna believe me, though."

But prison officials wouldn't let the reporter see him. If investigators talked to him—which they probably had—there was no record in the press. I dug deeper.

I found his registration card from WWI. I tracked him through census stats: living in Uniontown, southwestern Pennsylvania, with a nephew and a woman ten years his senior when he was 24, in

1920. I also found an unsolved beheading. It happened in 1921 in New Castle, north and west of Uniontown. More quickly turned up. Two around Fairmont-Monongah in the early '20s. One near Morgantown in 1926, in the Weirton Mine Section, in fact, very near where the coeds' bodies were found in 1970. Then more in New Castle in '28 and one in Uniontown in 1931.

In all, the killings lasted from 1921 to 1950 in a corridor from Monongah and Fairmont up through Uniontown to Pittsburgh and New Castle. In 1952 he went to prison for killing the two people in Fairmont. The unsolved beheadings stopped.

He was released in March of 1966, and there was another unsolved beheading in July. Then two in 1967, one in 1968, two in 1969. Then the coeds in Morgantown in January of 1970 and Cobun in Pendleton County in December. Hacker was arrested and the killings stopped again.

The kicker was that in the early part of the twentieth century, the Pittsburgh Seam, which ran from Uniontown to Monongah, was the highest producing seam of coal in the world. Rail lines between Monongah and Pittsburgh were the best available. Rockefeller, Camden, and Watson made sure that their interests were well serviced so the rape of the northern West Virginia mountains could proceed. A coal miner like Hacker could ride the rails with ease.

I didn't have anything close to proof, but Hacker appeared to have been one of America's first serial killers. As red light filtered into my study, I picked up the phone and dialed Matt's home number.

"Sergeant Hall," Matt said when he answered. He didn't sound like he'd been asleep recently. I wondered if he'd slept at all.

"This is some deep pile, Matt." I knew he suspected there were more killings, but I didn't think he would believe what I was about to tell him.

"How many?"

"About 23, near as I can tell, but that's not the main thing." Matt was silent, my cue to continue. "Hacker is 103 years old, and he's still alive."

* * *

It was half past noon when I pulled left off the main road onto the drive that led up to Sharpe Hospital. Six hours earlier, when I had told Matt Hacker was at Sharpe, he'd said he was going to see the man. I'd tried to get some shuteye, but by 10:00 had given up on that. I had to find out what happened.

Topping out at the parking lot, I saw the place was controlled chaos. A half dozen police cruisers, a couple local, a couple State. Sirens scattering blues and reds in every direction. I parked at the far end of the lot, got out.

As I approached, I was struck by the odd silence of the scene. People bustling here and there, but almost no one spoke. Crime scene tape surrounded a State Trooper's car in the eye of the storm. The license number read 62. Matt's cruiser.

I couldn't get close—stopped by a female officer who was patrolling the perimeter of the crime scene—but I edged around to see what was on the other side of the cruiser. A body lay face down on the pavement with a huge puddle of blood around the shoulders. Bodies bleed out much more than one would imagine. The fingers dug at the cement, one leg tucked up and under the body. . . . It was Matt. Officers were still assessing the situation.

I turned and marched into Sharpe. At the front desk, a man was nervously moving papers around, glancing toward the front door.

"What the heck happened out there?" I asked.

"I don't know." He sighed haltingly. "I just got on shift. An officer was leaving, and then the next thing I knew some woman ran in here screaming for me to dial 9-1-1."

"Jeez, that sucks," I said, resting a forearm on the counter. My heart was hammering. "I want to see my granddad. Hacker. Bill Hacker."

It's called pretexting, pretending to be someone you're not in order to discover information you're not supposed to know. It was something I was good at, but this time, I wish I hadn't been so convincing.

"Just a second." He scanned a list and then stabbed an intercom button. "Mr. Hacker? Your grandson's here."

There was a long silence before an old man's voice said, "Send the boy on up."

* * *

"I don't have no grandson." His voice was measured, soothing almost, with a strong southern lilt that had probably crept farther north in his day than it did at the end of the twentieth century. He was wearing wrist irons that were secured to the bed. A small man, but Hacker had forearms of corded and knotted rope. "You're with that Trooper."

I nodded. I didn't know what to expect, sitting in a chair in the bedroom of the man who might be America's most prolific unknown killer. The room was normal enough, standard hospice set up, oxygen tank beside the bed, but with very few personal touches. A single old daguerreotype of a young woman with tiny black eyes sat on a bedside shelf. Hacker saw me look at it and lay back, his eyes fixed on me.

"My mother." He rubbed his left palm down his cheek, and I saw he was missing his thumb and forefinger. His right hand was absent the forefinger. "What do you want to know? He okay, that Trooper?"

"Not at all," I said. "And you know what we think."

"Darn straight!" He clapped his hands together so sharply his wrist irons clanged. I flinched. He smiled. "I didn't kill nobody. 'Cept that jerk Estep in 19 and 52. Him and that whore Daliah. I did them. Had it coming."

I thought about mentioning his wife in 1937. "What about Sergeant Hall?"

He snorted. "Idiot. I warned him." Hacker tilted his head back and clacked his teeth together like some cats do when they're watching a bird.

"You killed him?" I was wondering how he got outside, how he overpowered a strong man who was a third his age. Hacker was shaking his head.

"Here's the skinny. Like I told that Hall guy." He passed his palms over open air, as if wiping the slate clean. "You ever heard of the Monongah disaster? Not the one in the sixties. The big one."

I nodded.

"When the number six exploded," he said, "the mine fan—thirty by thirty and solid concrete!—blew clear across the West Fork and imbedded in the hill, a hundred yards away. That was a big mother explosion." Hacker clacked his teeth again. "I was supposed to work that day—trapper boy—but I was puking my guts out from some kinda bad mushrooms that Stambouli and some of them wops had. Saved my sorry—"

"This was 1910 or something?"

"St. Nicholas's Day, December the 6th, 1907. It was bad."

I did the math. "Eleven years old."

"Wasn't many of us left for the clean up, I'll tell you what. Five hundred men died that day. Boys, too. Two buddies of mine, Cephus and Kyle, never came out. I had to help with the clean up. It was bad. They sent me in places adults couldn't get to."

"This is all fine, Mr. Hacker, but I'm trying to find out what happened to Sergeant Hall."

He sat back and his voice lowered. "He was your bud, wasn't he?"

"You could say that."

"Well, I'm sorry 'bout that. I warned him. If I go on, you could get infected, too."

He wasn't making any sense. "Sergeant Hall came to talk to you about—"

"I know what he came to talk to me about. You people think I killed all those people. Cut they heads off. But it ain't like that. Yeah, I was *involved*, just like this time, with Hall. But it wouldn't be right telling you how without saying there's a price comes for knowin'."

"Okay. I consider myself warned, Mr. Hacker."

He sat up, seemed positively enlivened. "Like I was saying, I was on clean up that day, after the explosions at Number 6 and Number 8. Talk about a Godawful mess! Smell like burnt flesh and afterdamp. . ."

He could tell that lost me and added, "The gasses that come after a methane explosion. Black damp, white damp, choke damp. You know.

"We was in there, looking after the bodies. When they couldn't go no further, they pushed me through a tangle of beams and black rock and all kinda crap. I had a little Wolf lamp, and those things ain't no darn good, but I got to a point where I could *see*. You know, somehow. Even though there was no light. Like those night cameras they got now."

"What did you see?"

"I saw a guy, sitting up just like you are, and he had a sandwich in his hand. Two bites gone. So was his head. We never did find it."

"His head. . . wasn't nearby?" I asked, already sickened by the turn this was taking.

"Never found it," Hacker said. "Or the others. The guy who was standing by a wall he just shot off—headless. Man on the tracks—headless. Lots of headless corpses. And no heads to be found. I crawled out. Reported back. They sent me right back in again. Said I was nuts or something, but I know what I saw. Couldn't take my eyes off it, like I was hypnotized." Hacker laughed dryly. "Later, they said it was the force of the blast. Told me not to mention it to anyone. Force of the blast? Screw that. Don't make no sense."

"So what do you think it was, Mr. Hacker?"

"Don't know," he said, shaking his head. "Some kinda *thing* formed by the explosion, all those deaths in an instant, is what I think. It follows me around since then. I've caught three so far," he said in a low voice. He looked around the room then, eyes darting about, and then lay back. His breath rushed out of him. "What happens is these lights, all glowy and dancing—like fireflies, only bigger. They buzz and they buzz and then there's this bright light, like an explosion, and then. . . ." He shrugged. "Dunno. Something. It follows me."

"Follows you?"

"The first was that New Castle woman in 1921, up near Pittsburgh. She was sweet on me. The lights nearly cut her head clean off. Then there was this guy in Pleasant Valley, outside of Fairmont. Pleasant, huh?" He snorted. "That's a joke."

I listened to his "confession" for nearly an hour. He accounted for all of the killings from 1921 through 1950 and then more from 1966 to the present. The lights had done it. An explosion of lights that, he said, matched the fury of the 1907 Monongah explosion.

"Why didn't you tell anyone before?" I asked.

"Weren't you listening? I told that woman who was sweet on me. The New Castle woman. Told that guy I was drinking with in Pleasant Valley. Told those two idiot coeds. None of them believed me. Not one."

I stood to leave soon after that, when it became clear he had nothing more. I extended my hand. Hacker shook it, held onto it a bit longer than was right.

"Thing is—and I know this now—those lights are going to find you," he said. "I know they will. I warned your bud just as I'm telling you now. Now that you know the story, you'll see them. Maybe today, maybe a year from now. If you don't believe, your head. . ." He drew his thumb sharply across his throat, his coal eyes holding mine. "But if you *do* believe, you'll see them, like me, but you won't die. Least I don't think so. You might wish for it, but you won't die. Look at me. I'm something over a hundred. You'll see me here in twenty years, I figure. Somewhere."

* * *

That night, I stood on my balcony with a glass of bourbon, wondering what had happened the last 36 hours. The skulls of two WVU coeds, decapitated almost thirty years before, had been found. A man who might or might not be America's most haunted serial killer had "confessed" with a story that might or might not be true. A. . . *spirit* unleashed by the Monongah coal mining disaster 93 years earlier. . .

In the driveway below, I saw what looked like a hundred fireflies swarming. Only bigger. Too big for fireflies. They whirred and swirled into a ball. I had the distinct impression they were focused on me. In that instant, I believed the curse of the 1907 Monongah disaster.

The lights dissipated, disappeared.

I wondered about the headless bodies in my future and the unnumbered headless bodies in the past. Mostly, I thought about Mared Malarik and Karen Ferrell, and how they died in the myth-shrouded hills of West Virginia.

Tim Waggoner

COUNTRY ROADS

Tim Waggoner's novels include *Forge of the Mind Slayers*, *Darkness Wakes*, *Pandora Drive*, *The Thieves of Blood*, the *Godfire* duology, *Like Death*, and *A Nightmare on Elm Street: Protégé*. He teaches creative writing at Sinclair Community College and is a faculty mentor in Seton Hill University's Master of Arts in Writing Popular Fiction program. Visit him on the web at www.timwaggoner.com.

Eric glanced at the digital clock on the dashboard and saw it was 3:38 A.M. He'd been driving all over Cabell County for almost three hours now, and so far the most interesting thing he'd seen was a raccoon. The animal had sat frozen in a ditch, staring at Eric's Altima as he drove by, eyes wide and shining bright as the light from the car's headlights washed over it. That was all: no deer, no coyotes, no other vehicles out cruising the back roads . . . and certainly not what Eric was searching for.

He reached for the thermos sitting in the cup holder, picked it up, and raised it to his mouth. The coffee inside had long ago gone cold, but it was strong and bitter, and full of caffeine, which was all that mattered. Eric was down to the dregs now, only a few swallows left at most. That, more than the length of time he'd been driving, made him consider giving up for the night and heading home.

And that's when he saw her.

She stood at the side of the road, draped in a sheer white outfit that might have been a dress, but might just as easily have been a nightgown. Her hair was long, black, and straight, and though it was windy tonight, both her gown and her hair remained still.

Eric eased his foot off the gas and slowly pressed down on the brake. In his rearview mirror, he saw the red glow of brake lights color the road behind his car, and he couldn't help thinking how eerie the light looked, like his Altima was wounded and trailing blood.

The woman's chalk-white complexion made her age difficult to determine. Eric guessed late twenties, early thirties, but she could've been anywhere from fifteen to forty-five. She stared straight ahead, expressionless and unblinking, like a life-sized porcelain doll. Just as he remembered her.

His heart pounded in his chest, and he felt a cold surge of fear at the base of his sternum. He clasped the steering wheel so tight his knuckles throbbed, and it took every ounce of self-control he possessed not to lift his foot off the brake, tromp down on the gas, and get the hell out of there. But he'd been searching for this woman for hours, and now that he'd found her, he wasn't about to flee, no matter how much he wanted to.

The Altima slowed to a stop next to the woman, and Eric put the car in park. He put his finger on the control to lower the driver's-side window, hesitated for a couple seconds, and then pressed it. The window receded into the door with an electronic hum.

The woman gave no sign that she was aware of him—she didn't lower her gaze to look at him, didn't move, didn't even appear to be breathing. Cool spring air wafted in from outside, bearing with it the sounds of insects and night birds. The noises seemed out of place, far too normal given the circumstances. It should be deathly silent, the air chill, and there should be a faint unpleasant odor like graveyard mold and bone dust. But Eric didn't smell any-thing other than the coffee on his own breath.

Now that he was here, now that he'd actually found her, he wasn't sure what to do . . . wasn't sure what he *wanted* to do.

"Uh . . . Hi. My name's Eric. Eric Montrose. I grew up around here, over in Huntington. I . . . I've seen you before. It was twenty years ago. Well, twenty-two, to be exact."

The woman continued staring straight ahead. No reaction at all.

"I had a friend, Joe Weidner. He and I used to drive around a lot on the weekends when we were in high school. We were both kind of shy, so neither one of us dated much, and there wasn't a lot to do except drive around and drink beer. There were no computer games back then, no satellite TV, no Internet . . . nothing else to do but drive, drink, and talk. We saw a lot of weird stuff out here late at night. Once we drove by a pasture, and a big animal was stand-ing at the fence watching us. I thought it looked like a horse with a skull head, but Joe said it didn't look like anything he'd ever seen before. One thing we did agree on, though. As we drove past, the thing *smiled* at us."

Eric shivered and forced out a laugh as if to dispel the mem-ory, but it just made him shiver harder.

The woman's catatonic expression didn't change, but Eric had the sense that she was listening to him. Or maybe that was just what he wanted to believe.

"Another time we saw a tree that was filled with dead ani-mals—possums, rabbits, weasels, foxes . . . Someone had skinned them and lodged them in the crooks of branches. The trunk of the tree was covered with strange symbols that had been carved into the bark. They looked like letters from a foreign language, but it wasn't one that Joe or I recognized. 'Course, it wasn't like either of us was exactly a genius in that department. We were both barely passing Spanish."

The woman still didn't lower her gaze to look at him, but Eric thought he saw a glimmer of reaction, a slight narrowing of her eyes, but he knew it could be his imagination.

"One Saturday night—prom night, as it turned out—we saw *you*. Neither Joe or I had dates. I'd been going out off and on with this one girl, Becky Schlosser, but it was one of our off times, and she went to prom with someone else. Joe and I talked about going stag, but we decided it would be too depressing, so we decided to just do our usual thing and go cruising. A lot of times when we went driving, we'd sit and listen to whatever song was on the radio, sip beer, and think our private thoughts. But other times we'd talk about stuff . . . which teachers bugged us, dumb things our parents or siblings did, girls we wished would look at us, let alone talk to us. A lot of times we wouldn't pay attention to where we were going, and we'd end up lost. That was part of the fun, not knowing where we were and trying to find our way back to town. Anyway, it was prom night when we drove down this road and saw you.

"It had rained earlier, and the roads were still shiny wet. We were both kind of depressed about missing prom—though we'd never have admitted it to each other—and we'd been drinking more than usual. I was driving that night, and I was concentrating extra hard on driving, you know, the way drunks do, and so Joe saw you first. 'Check it out, man!' he shouted. 'It's a girl!' At first I thought he was messing with me. We used to try to spook each other like that all the time. But sure enough, there you were, looking just like you do now, and I slowed down. I was driving an old beater Nova in those days, and the engine coughed and rattled like it was going to fall apart any minute. But despite all the noise my car made, you didn't pay any attention to us as we got closer.

"'Look at the way she's staring,' Joe said. 'You think she's crazy or something?' I told him that you might've been hurt or had suffered some kind of emotional trauma. I wanted to stop to see if you needed any help. But when I told Joe, he said, '*You're* the one who's crazy! I mean, look at her! She looks like some kind of ghost or vampire! And even if she is just a crazy person, what if she's got a knife or something and tries to kill us once we stop? Just keep going! We can call the police later!' And he grabbed hold of my right leg just above the knee and shoved my foot down on the accelerator.

"Nowadays, if I saw someone I thought needed help standing alongside the road, I'd call 911 on my cell, but nobody had cell phones back then. The only options we had were to either find a pay phone—and there sure weren't any out here—or stop at a farmer's house, pound on the door until he woke up, and ask to use his phone. Either way, it would be some time before any help could get out here, and by then it might be too late. I knew that, and I'm sure Joe did too, but we both felt a horrible sense of *wrongness* about you . . . though it had rained, you were dry, and though it was windy out—like tonight—your hair and gown didn't move in the breeze. You didn't look like you were blinking or even breathing. So it didn't take much for Joe to convince me to keep on driving. As we roared past, I checked the rearview mirror, half-expecting not to see your reflection, but there you were, still standing there, still not looking at us.

"We kept driving for about a half hour after that. Seeing you instantly sobered us up, but it took that much time for us to calm down. I convinced Joe that we should come back and look for you, just to make sure you weren't hurt, but we hadn't paid attention to what road we'd been on or how many turns we'd taken as we'd kept driving, and we couldn't find the right road again. We drove all night, and we didn't give up until close to dawn, and even then it was only because we were almost out of gas. We both got in big trouble when he got home. Both of our parents were sure we'd been out screwing around with a couple girls, and we let them think that. We knew they wouldn't have believed us if we'd told the truth.

"After that, whenever we talked about seeing you, we referred to you as our prom date. We asked around to see if any other kids had seen you, but no one had. I did some research in the town library on ghost legends and discovered that sightings of women in white have been common throughout history. Since I'd never heard of women in white before, that convinced me you were real. Joe wasn't so sure. He figured you might have just been someone who *had* heard of the legend, slipped on an old nightgown, and stood alongside the road to freak people out. I asked him why anyone would bother standing out in the country in the middle of the night when no one ever drove by. Joe said, 'We did, didn't we?' and that was the end of that."

Eric paused to drink the last of his tepid coffee. For a moment, he felt as if he should offer the woman in white a sip and the thought almost made him smile.

"I got a call from Joe's wife last week. He moved to San Antonio about ten years ago to work for a computer company there. He'd had a massive heart attack and died in his sleep. I live in Ohio now—I'm the manager of a Barnes and Noble there. I've got two teen-age daughters, an ex-wife, and more bills than I want to think about and, truth to tell, not much else. Joe and I kind of lost touch after high school, but once I learned he'd died, I started thinking about all those nights we used to drive these roads . . . all the things we talked about and all the things we saw. And I realized it had been a long time since I'd been home, and an even longer time since I'd been young."

He looked at the woman in white. He couldn't be sure, but he thought her head was angled slightly downward now, though her gaze still didn't meet his.

"I've been driving around out here all night looking for you. I'm not sure why. I just wanted to see you again, I suppose. Wanted to make sure you were real. Wanted to make sure that those nights twenty years ago were real. I guess memories are ghosts, too. But they don't haunt us with images of what used to be—they haunt us with reminders of the way things aren't anymore and can never be again."

The woman was looking at him now, though her eyes remained glassy and staring. He thought her bloodless lips twitched, as if she was about to say something, but she remained silent.

"Well, I guess I'd better get going." Eric pressed down on the brake and put the Altima in gear, but he didn't drive off right away. "This is probably going to sound weird, but . . . thanks. Thanks for giving me something to be scared of, to wonder about, for giving me hope that the world is more than just going to work, paying bills, and marking time until I die. Thanks for being a mystery." Eric smiled. "And for being my prom date."

As he raised the window, he wondered if the woman might

tap on the glass to get his attention, maybe open the door, reach in and grab him, or perhaps just materialize in the passenger seat next to him, morphing from woman in white to phantom hitchhiker. But she did none of those things, just continued standing there. Eric pressed down on the gas pedal and slowly pulled away. He tried to resist the urge to gaze in his rearview mirror, but he couldn't. When he looked, he saw the woman in white bathed in the red wash of his tail lights, patiently waiting for the next driver to come by who needed something to believe in . . . something to help carry him a little further down the road.

Mark Justice

THE WAY HOME

Mark Justice is the author of *Bone Songs*, a collection of stories from
Delirium Books, *Deadneck Hootenanny* (Novello Publishers) and, with
David T. Wilbanks, *Dead Earth: The Green Dawn* (PS Publishing). He also
hosts the nationally-recognized radio program *Pod of Horror*, available for
download at http://www.horrorworld.org/poh.htm. He lives with his
wife and cats in Ashland, Kentucky.

Clare saw the ghost for the first time on Tuesday night,
though she didn't know then what it was.

She hadn't been sleeping well for a few nights. This house
was old, and she wasn't used to the drafts and creaks and groans
that winter produced. Despite the new furnace, it could still get too
cold for her. Even now, in mid-March, she could be awakened by
the caress of cool air or a sound that made her think someone was
walking in the bedroom.

Drew, on the other hand, could sleep through anything.

At a little past two, she started awake, and thought, *Someone's here.* She lay silently, holding her breath until she determined
that no one was in the room, other than her slumbering husband. By
then, Clare was wide awake. She went down to the kitchen for a
glass of water. She sipped it in the dark, staring out the window at
their backyard, tinged in yellow by the security light over the
kitchen door.

Someone was standing in front of their storage building. A
boy. He was small, with black features, dressed in brown pants and

a stained shirt that was far too large for him. He was barefoot.

Clare nearly dropped her glass. What was a child doing outside at two in the morning, without shoes, in *March*?

She was sure no one could see into the house with the lights off, yet the black child seemed to be staring right at her. His expression was strangely adult, a sad resignation that was so palpable Clare imagined she could feel the weight of it even in the safety of her kitchen. It was the look someone had after they had been saddled with some particularly bad news, like the expression her father wore after the doctor calmly explained that the treatments weren't working and Clare's mother didn't have much more time.

The child lifted his arms like a baby reaching for its mother.

Clare blinked, and the boy was gone. He hadn't run—at least she didn't think so. He just disappeared.

She stood at the window for several minutes, trying to figure out what exactly she had seen. However, the longer she stood there, the more agitated she became, until she drew the curtains closed and turned on the kitchen lights. She checked the door locks and thought about climbing the stairs to the cold bedroom. Instead, she made coffee and worked puzzles in a Sudoku book until the sun rose and Drew came downstairs for breakfast. Thank God it was Saturday.

* * *

"His mom's probably a single parent, you know," Drew said. "Works two jobs. Maybe the kid's older sister is supposed to watch him or something, but her boyfriend drops over for a 'visit'. Nudge-nudge. Wink-wink." He went into his Monty Python accent, which was supposed to sound British but actually came off as drunken

Kentuckian.

Clare shook her head. "No. Maybe. I mean, there was something about him, something really sad. And the way he was dressed. . . I think he might have been abused."

Drew swallowed a spoonful of cereal. A drop of milk hung suspended on his lip, threatening to fall on his necktie. He was like a big, sloppy puppy, never letting anything get him down.

"Well, it shouldn't be too hard to find out who he is."

She knew he was right. Ceredo didn't have a large black population, which had been jarring for Clare. She had grown up in Philadelphia, where it seemed every race and creed were available within a few blocks of her family's townhouse. When she came to West Virginia for college she thought she would return to the big city after graduation, but then she met Drew, a big beefy Kentucky boy studying journalism and majoring in beer consumption. After the wedding, Clare got a teaching job in Huntington, while Drew went to work for the newspaper in Ashland, Kentucky, so they looked for a house somewhere in between. They ended up here in this small, quiet West Virginia town, just blocks from the Ohio River.

"I know who to ask," she said.

* * *

After Drew left for his Saturday shift at the paper, Clare did the grocery shopping. Lack of sleep made her eyes feel grainy and created a dull buzzing in her head, but she had been through worse in college.

When she unloaded the groceries back home, she saw Mr. Bordeaux on his front porch.

After the milk and apples and bread were stored away, she

crossed the street, thankful that he was still there.

"Mr. Bordeaux," Clare said. "How are you?"

"Tolerable." Mr. Bordeaux was in his nineties and looked every year of it. His face was lined with a wrinkle for every month of his life, it seemed. His eyes were yellow and rheumy. What little hair remained was a dirty white and stuck to his scalp as though it were damp. His liver-spotted hands held tight to a scuffed wooden cane. Mr. Bordeaux rocked slowly in a rusty glider. The squeak of the hinges sounded like old nails being pulled from a board.

"I wanted to ask you. . . That is, last night I saw somebody in my back yard—"

"John Joseph."

"Excuse me?"

"It's March. That's when John Joseph comes a-lookin' for his mama."

"I– I don't understand."

"He was a little colored boy, son of slaves. Went missing 'bout 18 hundred an' fifty after his mama and some other slaves got shot down right over there."

Mr. Bordeaux pointed at Clare's house.

"Wait." Her chest felt tight. "Slaves? Shot at my house?"

"House was part of the Underground Railroad," he said. "Was the Trammel house back then, my daddy tole me. The Baumgarner house over on Fifth was one of 'em, too. And the Randsdell Place."

"I've heard of the Railroad, of course, but I didn't know it operated in this part of West Virginia," she said.

"This was still Virginia back then." Mr. Bordeaux coughed and it went on so long Clare thought she might have to call an ambulance, but the old man finally got it under control and continued. "The Trammels kept it a secret for a long time, but folks eventually caught on. They was bringin' a slave family through in the middle of March when some men from town snuck up on 'em and shot 'em all dead."

Clare gasped.

"All but the boy. When they counted the bodies for the reward, John Joseph weren't there. At least that's what my great-grandpa said. He always claimed he shot the boy, but it must have only wounded him and he slipped off somewhere. Nobody ever saw him." Mr. Bordeaux smiled. His teeth were small and stained yellow, like his eyes. "'Cept anybody who lived in your house. Always this time of year."

Clare excused herself and went home. She could feel the goose bumps on her arms through the material of her coat.

That evening over dinner, she told Drew what Mr. Bordeaux had said.

"Yeah, right. He's such a reliable witness. You want to stay up for *Saturday Night Live*?"

Drew didn't make it to ten before he was snoring on the couch. She helped him up to bed, where she actually fell asleep for a few hours. When she opened her eyes, she was facing the door. A small figure stood there, silhouetted by the nightlight in the hall.

Clare nudged her husband. He rolled over and snored louder.

She climbed out of bed. The figure receded into the hallway.

Stepping into the hall, she whispered, "John Joseph?" She briefly glimpsed a shadow descending the stairs. She followed it down, vaguely aware that she should be more afraid.

She went out the kitchen door into the backyard. The boy was almost to the storage building. The structure was as old as the house, and the real estate lady had told Clare and Drew that it had been used as servants' quarters in the late 1800s.

The boy—John Joseph—stopped by the side of the storage building. He turned and stared at Clare. John Joseph appeared as substantial as she did. She could even see the mud splatters on his bare feet.

"What do you want?"

John Joseph lifted his arms to her. Clare reached for him, but the boy faded into nothingness. She fell to her knees as a sob escaped her lips. She was dressed only in her gown, but instead of the cold she felt only a terrible sadness.

Until she moved her head, allowing the light from the porch to illuminate the storage building.

Thick weeds grew in large clumps around the base of the structure. She grabbed a handful of them and tugged until the plants ripped away from the earth. In the gap she had created in the weeds, she saw it. There was a crawl space beneath the building. Too small for her, but maybe not for a child.

Clare ran back to the house. She pulled on a coat, boots and gloves, grabbed the keys to the building and a flashlight. She found a shovel in the storage building and carried it to the spot where John Joseph had vanished.

She dug.

When she thought she'd moved enough dirt, Clare lay down on the ground and reached under the building. It took her a minute, but she touched a cold object.

She removed a bone, the femur of a child.

It was wrapped in the remnants of brown cloth. Clare set it aside. Sighing, she resumed her prone position and reached under the storage building again.

It took nearly thirty minutes before the bones of John Joseph were recovered. Looking at the remains of the boy, Clare knew what had happened.

There was a large hole in the left collarbone, where John Joseph had been shot, possibly by an ancestor of Mr. Bordeaux. In the confusion—the screams, the smoke, the shouts of cruel men filled with bloodlust—the child crawled under the building and bled to death.

She touched the small skull. "Poor baby."

She began to cry.

A movement caught her eye.

Two figures stood only a few feet from her. The woman was tall, dressed in a threadbare coat. Next to her, holding his mother's hand, was John Joseph. He smiled at Clare.

For Clare, time stopped. There was nothing in the world, save for her and these two ghosts, dead for over one hundred fifty years.

The woman had high cheekbones and eyes that blazed even in the darkness. She studied Clare for a moment. She nodded, an unspoken gesture of thanks.

John Joseph released his mother's hand long enough to reach Clare. He pressed his small hand to her cheek.

His touch felt like snow falling on her skin.

John Joseph returned to his mother. The two walked away, hand in hand. Before reaching the neighbor's fence, they faded away.

Clare sat down next to the bones of the murdered slave child. She held her hand to the spot where John Joseph had touched her.

She stayed there for a while before she went back into the house to wake her husband.

Bev Vincent

SCREAMING JENNY

Bev Vincent is a contributing editor with *Cemetery Dance Magazine*, the horror industry's standard. His first book, *The Road to the Dark Tower*, an authorized companion to Stephen King's Dark Tower series, was published by *New American Library* in 2004 and was nominated for a Bram Stoker Award. He co-edited *The Illustrated Stephen King Trivia Book* with Brian Freeman for *Cemetery Dance Publications*. By day, Bev is a Ph. D. chemist with over thirty scientific publications. He is a monthly contributor to the Storytellers Unplugged blog and his official website is www.BevVincent.com

Pierce stared through the grimy windshield and thought about all the people he had killed in the past twelve years. Eight at least, and so many others maimed and ruined. Three of them had sought death at his hands, but the rest had simply had the misfortune of wandering too near his path.

He threw a switch. A single wiper blade pushed the dirt around in front of him. He dreamt about his victims all the time. He couldn't see their faces—had never seen them in life—but they haunted him just the same.

The others had warned him early on that it wasn't a question of whether he would kill, but when. That didn't make it any easier. Didn't stop the dreams.

Which was why he'd decided to quit. Give up the calls at all hours of day and night, demanding his immediate services. Give up the good pay and the greatest office on earth. The long trips that had kept him away from his wife and family so often that no one was waiting for him when he got back home any more.

He thought about buying a farm and hiring people to plant tobacco or whatever else grew around here, while he sat alone in his too-big ranch house and drank himself to oblivion. If he drank enough, his faceless victims might stop visiting him in the middle of the night.

He pulled the throttle back a notch, slowing the train.

Fowler, the conductor standing by his side in the locomotive's cabin, looked up from his clipboard and frowned. "There was no warning signal," he said. "We're green all the way."

Pierce nodded, but allowed the train to slowly lose momentum anyway. He didn't engage the airbrakes—he simply decreased the voltage from the diesel generator to the big electric motors that powered the axles.

Behind them, an unoccupied engine hooked up in tandem and ninety-six cargo cars with a combined weight of several thousand tons took up the slack in the knuckle couplers. The play in these couplers allowed the train to vary in length by up to sixty feet. An inexperienced engineer could break a train in two or damage the valuable freight by not properly controlling the slack. Pierce's job was to constantly read the track—curve, grade, and condition—in much the same way that Mark Twain's river pilots once read the mighty Mississippi.

Behind them lay Martinsburg and Duffields, miles of rolling farmland. Ahead, the mountains of Loudon Heights overlooking Harpers Ferry, the train tunnels leading to the Potomac crossing and Maryland beyond. Thomas Jefferson had once stood upon these peaks and said, "This scene is worth a voyage across the Atlantic."

The track approaching Harpers Ferry from the west was straight and level, but it had a reputation. Engineers were superstitious, and there were all manner of legends associated with trains, dating back to the brave phantom brakeman in the nineteenth century, to Casey Jones, whose reckless speeding cost him his life.

"We'll be late," Fowler said.

Pierce didn't reply, merely stared. Then he leaned forward against the console and squinted.

"What is it?"

Pierce flicked his index finger at the windshield, then slammed his hand against the emergency brake switch. "Hold on," he said, and braced himself.

Down the entire length of the train—over a mile—faster than the speed of sound, narrow rubber lines conveyed the urgent message to release air from each car's emergency reservoir. Hundreds of sets of brakes engaged, but it was a futile gesture. The area of contact between each wheel and the rail was smaller than a dime. Nozzles sprayed sand onto the track to increase braking traction, but even at fifty miles per hour, it would take over a mile for the train to come to a halt.

"What the—?" Fowler said, and then they were upon it. The crimson ball of flame that had been standing on the tracks exploded in a flurry of embers and sparks, but Pierce felt no more impact than would a car driver running over an empty soda can. Wheels locked, the train skidded down the tracks, leaving his latest victim in their wake.

Pierce grabbed the radio transmitter. "Dispatch. Train Q301. We hit someone on the tracks, approximately a mile west of Harpers Ferry. We are at full stop."

"You're kidding." the man on the other end said.

Fowler frowned and grabbed his own mike. "Fowler here. I saw it, too. Looked like someone on fire."

There was a long silence over the radio.

"Roger," the dispatcher said at last. "Please confirm that you wish to report striking a burning pedestrian on the tracks west of Harpers Ferry."

"I do," Pierce said.

"Roger that." Another pause during which Pierce could hear muffled conversation over the open channel. "We'll send out investigators and alert other traffic in the area of your situation."

"What was that all about?" Fowler asked. "Did I hear someone laughing?"

"You've never heard of Screaming Jenny?"

Fowler shook his head.

"Over a hundred and fifty years ago, after the Baltimore and Ohio Railroad was built, a woman living in an abandoned storage shed beside the tracks accidentally set her clothes on fire. A spark from her campfire, they say. She ran along the tracks screaming for help, probably heading for the station, but she was hit by a passing train. She would have died anyway—she was still burning when the engineer found her body."

Fowler looked at Pierce. "And you're saying . . ."

"Every now and then, especially when it's foggy, engineers report a burning figure on the tracks west of Harpers Ferry station."

Fowler stared open-mouthed a while longer, then shook his head. In Pierce's experience, he wasn't the sort of man who appreciated a good story.

By now, the train had finally squealed to a stop. "Let's inspect for damage," Pierce said.

"All the sensors show green," Fowler replied, pointing at the console.

"Computers will never see better than my own eyes," Pierce said.

Before Fowler could respond, Pierce had navigated the narrow corridor behind the cab and climbed down the eight-foot ladder to the ground. Computers would never be haunted by visions of the dead and maimed either, he thought.

Fowler followed a few seconds later. He trudged toward the back of the train. The engine was Pierce's responsibility—everything else belonged to the conductor. Before the advent of electronics that sensed the position of each car relative to switches and junctions, the conductor stayed at the back in a little red caboose. Now they rode together in the front cab, the conductor calling out signals and reminding the engineer of slow orders.

The sun was dropping over the back of the train, and the air was crisp and cool. The sound of the idling diesel engine reverberated off the tree-covered hills on both sides of the track. Pierce headed to the front of the locomotive and examined the nose coupler. Besides bird feathers and the remains of countless insects, he found a shred of scorched cloth wedged into a crevice. The front of the train was spattered with blood and gore.

"Steady where you're at, mate," a voice said from behind.

Pierce froze.

"Your name, please."

"Edward Pierce."

"Good name," the man said. "Turn around slowly and keep your hands where I can see them."

Pierce obeyed. The stranger had a thick black beard, wore a heavy, dark coat, and carried a rifle.

"Where's the conductor?"

"Checking the rest of the train."

The man nodded. "We'll hang out here for a while. My colleagues will join us shortly."

"What did we hit? Was that a real person on fire?"

"Someone no longer in need of her mortal remains. Effective, no?"

Gunshots rang out from behind Pierce, toward the back of the train. More faceless phantoms to blot out with bottles of whisky and bourbon on his new farm. He wondered if Fowler was the victim or if the robbers had killed the armed guards in the innocuous freight car near the middle of the train. He also wondered how long it would take for the authorities to show up, but he couldn't risk checking his pocket watch.

"Won't be long now," the man with the gun said, as if he'd been reading Pierce's thoughts.

Pierce's wife had moved to Maryland after the divorce, taking their two children. Sometimes she brought them to him at the end of one of his runs and they had a day together at the park or the zoo, but not often enough. Maybe they'd visit him on his farm, on days when he put away the bottle and tried to imagine what it would be like to have a family again.

Several minutes later, Pierce heard footsteps on the gravel beside the tracks. "Done," the newcomer said. Pierce didn't turn—the fewer faces he saw, the better off he'd be in the long run.

"The conductor?" the man with the gun said.

"Tried to be a hero," the voice behind Pierce said.

"You have it all?"

"Ready to go. There's a railcar about three thousand yards down the tracks heading this way. They'll be here in a minute or two."

Pierce heard footsteps receding behind him.

The man reached inside his coat and pulled out a slip of paper. He handed it to Pierce. "Accounts and access codes. Everything you'll need to get your money."

Pierce clutched the page and scanned the strings of digits. His retirement fund. Enough money to buy a farm, hire labor and keep the liquor flowing. Enough to guarantee his children a good education. He folded the sheet and tucked it behind a picture of his kids in his wallet.

"Pleasure doing business," the man said. He raised his hand to his forehead and pretended to doff his non-existent hat. "Sorry about this, but it's for your own good." He raised the rifle and smashed the stock into the side of Pierce's head.

By the time Pierce regained consciousness, the men were gone and the investigators from Harpers Ferry were calling for reinforcements. Today's run was supposed to end in Baltimore but Pierce doubted he'd get there any time soon. He knew he had difficult days ahead of him, answering questions from cops and probably from federal agents once everyone figured out what had been stolen, but it would be worth it. Aching head and all.

He could already picture the sweeping green fields from his back porch. Each night he would say a prayer for those who had been lost on his watch, and another for the soul of Screaming Jenny, who had come to his rescue.

Marta Murvosh

SMOKE AND STEEL

Marta Murvosh is a journalist in Northwestern Washington. She was born in Las Vegas about the time the original Star Trek series launched. One of her first memories is watching a lunar landing on television. That historic event, along with seeing Planet of the Apes at an impressionable age, started her on a love affair with speculative fiction. Her father earned money during college at Weirton Steel. *Smoke and Steel* is her first published fiction story.

The fiery glow from the furnaces of Weirton Steel reflected off tiny metal slivers suspended in the dank air. As Joe drove on Route 22 from Pittsburgh down the plateau into town, it was like descending into Hell. The belch of hydrogen sulfide from the mountains of slag surrounding the steel mill stank like the Devil's own outhouse. It was the smell of Weirton, both the steel mill and the town of the same name. It was the smell of a place that measured success in rolls of carbon steel sheets. Smoke and steel were what Joe knew, but lately success was a stranger, as fleeting as the flickering lights of the ghost.

Maybe that's why the ghost stayed at the mill, Joe thought as he parked in the company lot in Larry's sedan. When you spend your life breathing smoke and steel, moving on might be hard. As the time clock clunked down on his timecard, Joe figured an afterlife resembling a revival preacher's tale of brimstone wasn't near as pleasant as sweating through a double in the open-hearth. Of course, Joe wasn't convinced that the weird moans and the flickering lights really were signs of a ghost anyway.

Fear of a Devil he hadn't met kept Joe working at Weirton Steel as a watchman four years after he'd broken his back in a mill accident. He'd lost his livelihood, his wife, and his house. Black Friday ended any hope of work elsewhere. Joe put Larry's car keys in the slot next to the older man's time card. He'd have to remember to thank him at lunch. He wondered if Larry'd checked on that hole in the yard fence they had patched last week. Joe stowed his lunch pail filled with apples, leftover fried chicken, and coffee that his sister-in-law had packed. He began his rounds.

About four hours into his shift, Joe walked into the huge building that housed the No. 2 furnace, where he liked to remember his days as first helper. Back then, when he gazed through blue goggles into the blast furnace, Joe could tell the exact temperature of the demon's mouth, just by the color. He, not the guy with the fancy thermometer, decided when the ladle of molten steel was ready to pour into the molds. Joe had been the one to say it was time for the crane to lift the fiery bowl of liquid metal. Now, the No. 2 hearth was as cold as the banker who foreclosed on Joe and his family while he was flat on his back.

The scrape of shoe leather on the ground broke the hearth's silence. Joe's ears perked up and he pointed his flashlight into the hearth's corners. Penny-pinching Old Man E. T. Weir didn't want his watchmen using any power in the No. 2 building while the furnace was shut down. Joe didn't see anything and turned to leave. He figured he'd dawdled enough in his memories and had better check the fence to see if the patch covered the hole. Pipes gurgled, but the brush of cloth on dolomite-lined firebrick drew Joe back to peer around the furnace.

A shadow exploded from behind the hearth, knocking Joe to the ground. His back hit the floor hard. The flashlight skittered across the floor. He cried out for the fleeing figure to stop.

"Ayeiii," the shadow screamed. It flew past Joe toward the door, feet tapping out a foxtrot.

Pain jackknifed Joe. His shout broke into a screech. Flashing lights blasted pinwheels into his eyes. For a moment he thought he saw the furnace on fire with a ladle of molten steel ready to go. Heat hit Joe. He could hear the first helper, a tall man, shouting at him to get to work.

They say when a man falls into the ladle of molten steel, his body explodes instantly. At times like this, Joe wished he'd fallen into the liquid steel, rather than ending up at the bottom of a load of dolomite.

When the hurt passed, Joe gasped and floundered, a turtle flipped on his shell. The pipes gurgled, lights flickered, and Larry's crotchety voice called to the ghost. "Hank, cut that crap out."

Larry was on speaking terms, so to speak, with the ghost. As the stomp of Larry's work boots grew closer, Joe cleared his throat and tried to shout. "Larry, help!"

His voice broke, but Larry had pretty sharp ears for an old guy, and in a few strides, the retired mill foreman was at Joe's side, bringing with him the smell of peppermint gum.

"What happened?"

"Tramp hiding in the blast furnace." Joe gasped. "Knocked me for a loop. I was seeing things. Can you help me up?"

It'd been years since Larry shoveled coke into the open hearth, but he was still built like a stevedore. Soon Joe was on his feet, urging Larry to help search for the tramp.

"Weren't no one coming out here when I was on my way in," Larry said, peering around an empty metal bin. "You sure it wasn't Hank? He's been a bit ornery tonight."

Joe's brows narrowed. "Larry, ghosts don't wear shoes."

Larry nodded, picked up Joe's lantern and began to search the room. "How was your visit with your kids?"

Joe sighed as he looked behind a shelf. Since his wife Flo had died, his sister-in-law, Stella, and her husband, Ray, were raising Joe's four children in Pittsburgh. When he visited, Joe felt like the days were spent measuring the distance between his boys and himself. The littlest, just two, had to be reminded sometimes that Joe, not Ray, was his dad.

"Getting big," Joe told Larry. "Thanks for the loan of your car. I'll get you some gas come payday."

"Don't worry about it. I'm grateful you're driving it more than just around town."

Behind the furnace, Joe saw a small suitcase wrapped with frayed rope. He grunted as he stooped to pull it out and winced when the pain in his back caught him. "Larry, get a load of—"

Something metal clattered in the hallway.

"That ain't Hank," Larry said.

Heck no, Joe thought. Larry took the lead. "Hold up," the old man shouted, his boots thumping as he sprinted into the yard.

When Joe caught up to Larry, he found him standing over a wraith of a man. Covered in ash, the trespasser shook. The shape of the tramp's hands covering his face owed more to bone than flesh.

"We don't want to hurt you none," Larry was telling the tramp. "We just can't let you stay here, son. We'd lose our jobs."

The tramp dropped his hands. He was a young man, but his

skull stood out like he'd been five years in the grave.

"The furnace is haunted," the tramp said. "A man died there, exploding. He's just smoke and steel. Smoke and steel."

Joe shook his head and looked at Larry, who asked, "Son, when's the last time you ate?"

"Don't know," the tramp whispered. "Ghost ate me. There's a fire in the furnace you know."

"I'll get you some food. Sit tight," Joe said. He shuffled to the lockers and retrieved his lunch pail. As he approached the No. 2 building, lights flickered in the doorway. Darn faulty wiring. He hoped no one could see it and tell Old Man Weir. If the mill owner heard about the lights, he'd dock their paychecks just to keep a few pennies in his own pocket.

When Joe returned to the yard, Larry introduced him to the tramp.

"This here's Bill," Larry said. "He worked at some mills in Virginia. He says he mostly walked here. I think he's the guy dayshift ran off. He must have snuck back in through that hole in the fence."

Joe introduced himself and reluctantly peeled the wax paper from the fried chicken leg that Stella had carefully packaged for him and offered it to the tramp. The man grabbed it and began to gnaw through Stella's crisp buttermilk batter. Joe knew it was tasty, just like Flo used to make. The tramp's eyes lost their crazy gleam.

"Much obliged, sir." The gratitude in his voice made the loss of the fried chicken easier for Joe to bear.

Joe nodded and gave Bill one of the apples from his in-laws' garden. He had more in his locker to give his landlady at the boarding house toward his rent.

"You still seeing Hank?" Larry asked. Joe guessed that Larry had told Bill about the ghost.

"No, sir. I was talking crazy, wasn't I?" Bill said rhetorically. "Hunger must've made me see things."

"Well, you're lucky we found you," Larry said. "Someone on day shift might have roughed you up to impress Old Man Weir. When you ran into Joe here, I almost figured you for Hank. Sometimes that ghost has one too many at the bar and raises a ruckus."

Bill smiled weakly. "You know where I can find work? I haven't had a job in two years."

Joe shook his head. "Ain't no work here."

"Across the river in Steubenville, Mrs. Moore, she'll feed folk, if they help her with some yard work," Larry said. "She's the third house past the Russian Church. She's got a big garden. You can't miss it."

"Thank you, sir," Bill said.

Larry gave Bill a hand up, and he and Joe walked the man out the mill's gate. They directed Bill toward the Fort Steuben Bridge. Then Larry suggested that he and Joe split the sandwich his wife had packed for lunch.

As they ate, Larry wanted to speculate on Bill's prospects, but Joe didn't, and he tuned his coworker out. Bill might not have a job, but he could still do hard work. Joe imagined racing after Bill, catching the tramp before he got to Mrs. Moore's home and kicking him down, down as low as Joe was now. Joe's legs stung with the impact of imagined blows.

"You should go, too," Larry said.

"Go to Mrs. Moore's? I'm already rooming there." For a moment, Joe was confused. "Widow Moore can handle that boy. She knows how to lay down the law."

"You weren't listening to me," Larry said. "You've gotta go, get out of the mill."

"Why?" Joe asked. "It may not be full time, it may not pay well, but it's work."

"Hank isn't the only one haunting the mill. Joe, you slink around here like a phantom. Your spirit is skinnier than that boy we just rousted. You need to get out of Weirton Steel and this town before you fade away."

"Who are you to talk to me like that?" Joe shouted. "You may have been my boss when I started working here, but you aren't now. Did the bank take away your house? Did your wife die? No. You worked long and hard, paid off your house and kept your money in a mattress. They can't take that away, like the Crash took away my life's savings and the bank took my house and cancer took Flo."

Joe wanted to smash Larry's face in, striking as hard as life had struck him down. His arm swept his lunch pail off the table. It clattered as it hit the floor. He kicked it across the lunchroom.

Larry nodded calmly as if Joe hadn't thrown a fit. Ashamed, Joe winced. Pipes gurgled. Lights flashed.

Joe picked up his pail. As he stowed it in his locker, Larry cleared his throat and poured another cup of coffee.

"It's not right, you working here and your kids up in Pittsburgh," Larry said. "Didn't you say your sister-in-law's husband might have work?"

"Maybe." Joe grunted. He thought he might be able to help out at his brother-in-law's dry cleaning business, but Joe reckoned his in-laws didn't need one more person to provide for. "Larry, smoke and steel's always been my life. It's the Devil I know."

The lights flashed again, distracting Joe from his depressing thoughts.

"Cut that out, Hank," Larry said. "We don't need no trouble from Mr. Weir."

Joe stood up. "We better get back to work before someone tells Old Man Weir we took too long to eat."

Joe went into the No. 2 furnace building and tried playing with the light switches, hoping to locate the loose one. Maybe the vibrations from the No. 1 furnace caused the flicker. The pipes gurgled. The lights flashed.

The furnace roared to life. Joe threw up his hands to ward off the heat. Where were his gloves? Where were his goggles to keep his eyes from burning?

It was hotter than he remembered, and the crane stood ready to lift the huge ladle liquid steel. Already sweat soaked through his T-shirt and the long-sleeved canvas shirt he wore to protect himself from sparks. The foreman beckoned him over. He was a tall, skinny man, and like Joe, he wore a layer of long johns under his jeans to protect himself from the sparks and wave of heat. His name patch read *Henry* and his face looked kind.

"Joe, where've you been? We've been missing you."

"Been hurt, boss," Joe said.

"Smoke and steel, it burns you quick or slow," the foreman said as the lights flickered. "What's it going to be?"

The furnace grew hotter. Even without his goggles, Joe could see the steel was ready to pour. He thought about his boys, about his weary muscles, his painful life. Joe shook his head. The steaming ladle dwarfed Joe, but Hank stood tall, ready to direct the crane.

"This one's yours, if you want it," the ghost said. "There's another one ready in the No. 1 furnace."

Coke and iron coated the back of Joe's dry throat, more smell than taste. Coal-black grime stained the skin under his fingernails, just as it had discolored his father's hands. Joe had always thought his sons would follow him into the mill, breathing in the damp, dusky Ohio River air tinged with smoke and steel. He began to cough and couldn't stop, hacking as if his lungs could expel all his pain and fear. He doubled over and fell. Hank stood over him, and Joe's legs twitched feebly, trying to kick the ghost.

"What's it going to be, Joe?"

"I'll go slow, Hank," Joe whispered. "I want to see my boys grow up."

Then the ghost was gone, and the furnace was cold. Joe lay shivering on the floor with his eyes closed until Larry found him at the end of their shift.

Brian J. Hatcher

THE HUNGRY EARTH

Brian J. Hatcher lives in Charleston, WV, and refers to himself as a dedicated and unrepentant raconteur. Brian is a writer, poet, oral storyteller, actor, magician, fire-eater, and indy wrestling manager. Brian also enjoys delving into the technical side of things. He serves as the webmaster for both his website (http://www.brianjhatcher.com) as well as the website of poet Brandy Schwan (http://www.grimtrixter.com).

Bill Walls listened to Doris Winters busying herself in the kitchen. She whistled blissfully, the plates clanking as she pulled them from the cabinet. She had no idea.

Bill knew it had to be done, but he still felt sorry for her. He wondered how she would take it. Would she keep her dignity, or would there be tears and screams? And would she know the men she welcomed into her home today would be the ones responsible?

Bill sat in an old wooden rocker in the corner of her living room, its arms pressing into his sides and creaking each time he nervously shifted his weight. Coffee cooled in a cup in his right hand, untouched.

Mrs. Winters carried in a plate of fresh-baked sugar cookies. She offered Bill one, which he refused with a raised hand, then she took a seat on the couch next to Jack Reagan, Bill's boss.

Bill could barely look in her direction, but Jack chatted away as if she was an old family friend. But the friendly conversation, to Bill, seemed. . . ominous.

"I don't get many visitors," Mrs. Winters said to Jack. "People don't have a reason to come up this way since the mine closed. That's why I set my trailer here, for the privacy. That, and to be closer to Tom."

"Your husband?" asked Jack.

"Yep. Been gone twenty-nine years now."

"The cave-in, right?"

Mrs. Winters cocked her head. "You know about that?"

Jack sipped his coffee. "Yes, ma'am. My father died in the same cave-in."

Bill cringed and hoped Mrs. Winters hadn't noticed.

Mrs. Winters placed her hand on Jack's shoulder. "I'm so sorry. You were close to your father?"

"I didn't get a chance to know him. I was only three when he died. I can't remember what he looked like and Mom didn't have pictures of him. He's as good as a stranger to me."

"A boy shouldn't have to grow up without a father," said Mrs. Winters.

"Mom did all right. She took care of me, I have no complaints."

"So that's why you want to go up to the old mine? To see your Dad?"

Jack frowned. "What do you mean? They recovered all the bodies. Dad's buried in Charleston."

"And Tom's body is buried in Beckley. But he's not there under that piece of stone with his name carved in it. His soul, the part of him I loved, is still down in that mineshaft. Has been since the cave-in. Sometimes at night, when the wind blows down from the mountain, I can hear his voice whispering in it. And the others, too."

"You mean the mine's—"

Mrs. Winters smiled. "Go ahead. You can say it. I know the truth of it."

"Haunted?" asked Jack.

"Every mine is haunted, dear, in one way or another. A mine shaft is a hole in the earth, an emptiness needing to be filled. The emptiness makes the earth hungry, and it eats whatever it finds.

"Sometimes the earth will close up its throat and take men whole, like it did my Tom and your father. Most times though, the earth steals just a little bit of a man, not enough at first to notice. Tom worked in the mines thirty years before he died, and I was married to him for nearly as long. I could see it in his face, in his eyes, more and more every day. My Papa was a miner, and I saw the same thing happen to him.

"It wasn't just being tired or old. It was like a small piece was gone. A piece of his soul. That's what happens. The mine eats a man's soul, one piece at a time."

Jack took a deep breath. "That might be true. But I wasn't going up there to find ghosts. I just wanted to see the mine for myself, the place that took my father."

"You might find more than that, if you really want to. When are you planning on going?"

"Not today. Soon, though."

"It isn't hard to find. My trailer is right in the middle of the old access road. You can still see where it ran up the hill from my back porch. I used to walk up there every once in a while and lay flowers at the mouth of the old shaft for Tom. But this old body of mine's gotten too tired to make the climb. When you decide to go up, stop by here first. I'll give you some flowers to take to Tom, if you don't mind."

"Not at all."

"Thank you. And when you come back down, I'll have fresh coffee waiting for you."

"I really appreciate that." Jack stood. "It's getting late. Bill and I better get going."

Finally. Bill worked himself out of the rocker and set the still-full cup of cold coffee on the coffee table.

Mrs. Winters shook Jack's hand. "I'm really glad you stopped by. Sometimes I forget how lonely I am." She touched Bill's arm. "It was nice meeting you too, young man."

Bill couldn't look her in the eye. "Thank you."

"Your friend don't talk much, does he?" she asked Jack.

"Actually he does, too much for his own good sometimes. Fortunately, you were spared most of it."

"He likes to pick at you, huh?" she asked Bill with a wink.

"I'm used to it."

Mrs. Winters opened the door to let them out. "I enjoyed our talk, Jack. I hope you'll be back by soon."

Jack smiled. "I figure I will."

Bill and Jack walked down the steep gravel road to the bottom of the hill. Bill didn't want to scratch or ding up his new truck, so he insisted they park at the bottom and walk up. He didn't speak or look Jack's way for a while.

"She was a nice lady," Jack said finally.

"What are we doing here? How could you just sit there, eat her cookies and drink her coffee, all the time knowing you're putting her out of her house in less than a week?"

"I'm not putting her out of her house, the company is. If you want, you can try to talk them out of it."

"Look, nobody told that lady to park her trailer in the middle of the access road. Whether or not the company wanted to re-open that mine, she's still trespassing. But that's not the point. Why come up here in the first place?"

"I needed to know if this was the right mine."

"The maps in the Assayer's Office could've told you that."

"They couldn't tell me everything I needed to know."

"That's a load of crap, Jack, and if you want to know the truth of it, pretty cold-blooded."

"Believe what you want. And I'm sorry you were so uncomfortable up there, but the sooner you realize that decisions you make don't just change numbers on a ledger but affect real people, the better off you'll be."

Bill unlocked the truck, and they both climbed in. Bill put the key in the ignition, but didn't start the engine. "Before you decide to ride off on that high horse of yours, let me ask you something. That 'nice lady' would've told you all the ghost stories you wanted to hear, even if she knew your father was really a retired steelworker living in Florida. Why did you lie to her?"

Jack turned away and stared out the window. "Let's get out of here."

* * *

"What are you trying to do, wear a hole in my carpet?" asked Jack. "I must have heard you go past my office door at least twenty times."

"Can you blame me?" asked Bill.

"Well, get in here."

Jack rarely kept his office door closed. That he closed it during the conference call with the head office worried Bill. That Jack was closing it behind him now as he sat down in front of Jack's desk really scared him.

"So?" asked Bill. "Are we still in business or what?"

Jack sat down behind his desk. "Everything checked out. The Union reps didn't find anything. There won't be any strike."

"That's it?"

"We're back in business. What more do you want?"

"I want to know why we're not breaking out the champagne right now. This is supposed to be good news, right? What are you so down about?"

"Do you really think the miners will go back to work like nothing ever happened?"

"Why not? The Union says the mine's safe."

"The safety concerns were just a delaying tactic. It's not the real issue and you know it."

Bill slumped in his chair. "We're not going to start this again, are we? I've had it up to here with listening to ghost stories."

"Who's been telling you ghost stories?"

Bill was startled by Jack's sudden eagerness. "Nobody. I just overheard some of the men talking. It's no big deal."

"What did they say?"

"Nothing."

"No, you said you've heard ghost stories. What kind of stories?"

"You serious?"

Jack shot up from his chair. "No, I'm talking to hear myself talk. What did they say? They hear chains rattling? They see floating sheets wearing miner's hats? What?"

"Whispers. They heard whispers."

Jack sat back down. "Like what Mrs. Winters said she heard."

"It's just a coincidence. You don't really think there are ghosts down there, do you?"

"You're missing the point. We're asking the men to go down that shaft, and they don't want to. Sure, we can make them. But then what do you think the production numbers will look like? And who do you think the head office is going to blame?"

"All the more reason to crack down."

Jack shook his head. "We turn this into a war, we'll lose in the end."

"What other choice do we have?"

"We need to show the men that everything's all right, and we have to show we're willing to stick our own necks out to prove it. I'm going to inspect the mine myself."

"But the Union reps have already done that."

"Only the main shaft. Not Shaft 22, the site of the cave-in."

"That's because no one's working that shaft. It's closed off."

"If I go down there, by myself, maybe the men will be willing to follow."

"If they don't want to go down there after the Union's said it's safe, they sure won't just because you went into 22. You want to have an exorcism? Call in the Ghosthunter guys? Fine, do it. But you going down there won't make a difference."

"I gotta try, Bill."

"You know something? You've been acting weird ever since you became mine manager. Talking to Mrs. Winters just made it worse. Look, I've known you since high school. You didn't used to be like this. You used to be tougher."

"More domineering, you mean."

"I mean you paid more attention to the bottom line. That's how you got as far as you have. You knew what was important. A year ago, you would have threatened layoffs and not thought twice about it. Now you want to coddle the men? It won't change anything. And we still have to get our numbers up."

"You've had your nose in the ledger books for too long. Numbers aren't more important as people."

"The hell they're not. If those numbers aren't up, then everyone goes hungry. Everyone."

"And that's why I have to do this. Maybe I am wasting my time, and if it doesn't work, then we declare war. I won't have much of a choice then. But I have to know I tried everything else before I drop the hammer."

"I'm asking you. I'm begging you. Don't go down there."

"You afraid the ghost'll get me?"

"You can't jump every time the men have a complaint. If it isn't this, it'll be something else. There will always be ghosts. There's nothing you can do about that."

"Bill, I honestly don't know if there is such a thing as a ghost. But Mrs. Winters was right about one thing. A mine does eat a man's soul a piece at a time. Don't you get it? That's what we're asking the men to give up for us. Why they do it, I don't know, except they have families to feed. Is it too much to ask for me to go down there for the men who give up their souls for us?"

"And what will you do when you lose your own?"

* * *

135

"Why did you say that?" Sergeant Parks' brow furrowed, as if checking off items on a mental list.

Bill leaned back in his office chair. "I don't know why I said it. It just seemed like I was looking at him for the last time."

"But you did see him later that evening."

"He was walking up to the building as I pulled out of the parking lot. I waved, he waved back."

"Did you see the pistol?"

"I had no idea he owned a gun, much less had one with him. With that heavy coat he was wearing, he could have been carrying in an arsenal, and I wouldn't have seen a thing."

"Didn't you think it strange he was wearing so heavy a coat in late August?"

Bill smiled. "He was going into the mine. Sun doesn't make it down there too often, gets kind of cold."

"Yes. Of course."

"But that was the last time I saw him, until they hauled his body out of the mine."

"Did he seem suicidal?"

"No. His life was good, and he seemed really happy, at least until we started working the mine. I thought something might happen, but—"

"But?"

"But the facts speak for themselves, I guess."

"But why do it in the mine? And why did he wait four hours?"

"So you don't think it was suicide?"

"Until I get all the facts, I'm not formulating any theories."

"C'mon, you have to have at least a couple. If it isn't suicide, what was it? I did get promoted to Jack's position when he died. Doesn't that throw up some sort of red flag for you?"

"And do you think just because you said that, that puts you in the clear?"

"No, I don't. But I am about to punch a hole in your theory. I just quit."

"You did?"

"That's right. The only reason you found me at the office today is because I'm getting the last of my things."

"Why did you quit?"

"Personal reasons." Bill stood up from his chair and picked up a cardboard box of his things from his desk and placed it under one arm. "I know you want a nice, tidy explanation, but I don't think there's one to be had. Jack killed himself, and you're never going to know why. Even I don't know, really. I have theories, but nothing you'll be able to put into a report."

"Tell you what. You tell me your theories, and let me figure out how to put it in the report."

"Yeah, good luck." Bill glanced at his watch. "Time to get out of here. I'll tell you what. Grab that other box and carry it to my truck, and we'll talk on the way. I don't stay here after dark."

"Why?"

"Part of the story."

Bill and Sergeant Parks left the building. Bill locked the door, and they walked across the gravel parking lot.

Bill asked, "Did you know Jack's father died in that mine? I didn't. I thought Jack's dad lived in Florida. I didn't know it was his stepdad."

"Why would he want to work the mine, then?"

"I'm not even sure he knew. He played the whole thing by ear. He was looking for something, and I guess he found it. I don't think he necessarily planned to kill himself. But he took the gun because he knew there was that possibility."

"What do you think he was looking for?"

"His dad's ghost. When Mrs. Winters told Jack his dad was down that mineshaft, he might not have believed it at first, but he started to. I can see it now, looking back at it. It explains everything. I guess, in a way, his dad's been haunting him his whole life. And he killed himself, not because he wanted to die, but to be with his dad forever. In that shaft."

"Then why the four-hour wait?"

"Because he wasn't going to do it unless he was absolutely sure his dad was down there."

"You mean he saw his father's ghost."

"He *believed* he saw his father's ghost. That was enough."

Bill climbed into his truck. He rolled down the window. "You still plan to go down into the mine?"

"I need more than just a ghost story to close this case."

"And I'm sure the company would like a nice tidy explanation so they can open up the mine again. I think you're better off not looking for it, though."

"It's my job, Mr. Walls. But let me ask you one more thing. Honestly, what do you believe happened down there?"

"Nothing happened down there."

"That's what you believe?"

"That's what I choose to believe. What Jack saw or didn't see, I don't care to think about. But I will say this. When I told Jack I had overheard the men say they heard whispering, I was lying.

138

I'm the one who heard it.

"About a month ago I was leaving late from work, it was almost midnight. I was in the parking lot and I heard something. A sound coming off the mountain. Whispering in the wind, just as Mrs. Winter's described it. And I haven't stayed here after dark since. Maybe I was imagining it then. Or maybe I'm deluding myself now. But I'll tell you this. If I were to hear Jack's voice whispering in the wind, I don't know what I'd do. And I don't want to know."

Bill started the engine. "Let the dead rest, Sergeant. They're where they belong. Let everybody tell all the haunted mine stories they want, like it even matters. There's nothing in that mine now but the dead. The dead feed the earth, you know. But the earth's still hungry. It's always hungry."

Jude-Marie Green

WILD MOUNTAIN FREESIA

Jude-Marie Green has been an astronaut**, plumber**, show-horse trainer*, PTA mother*, recognized fabrics artist*, marathoner*, sky-jumper**, and astronomer**. Still she manages to write fiction that is even more fantastic than her life.

Living in Southern California with her cats and books, she watches too many movies and reads too many books, resulting in stronger eyeglass prescriptions every year. She is considered an emerging fantasist, with short-fiction sales to Say, *Why Aren't We Crying?*, *Abyss & Apex*, *Ideomancer*, and *Visual Journeys*. She is also an assistant editor (and review columnist) for *Noctem Aeternus Magazine*. And she longs to be Stephen King when she grows up.*

*Very true.
**Not so true.

"Stomach cancer!" the woman in the back seat said. "All that black boy did was touch me and he died of stomach cancer!" She paused. "At least they didn't lynch him."

My driver's license says my name is Fred Lytle, that I'm 19, that I live in Logan, West Virginia, but it doesn't tell ya what a careful driver I am. I've been driving since 15 1/2 with my folks' permission. I was out of high school and working to win that safe driver certificate sponsored by my insurance company. I bought my own first car, a second-hand Saturn rather than a friend's tricked-out ancient Camaro, because I wanted to be safe. So of course I knew better than to pick up hitchhikers but this woman—petite, delicate, beautiful as a field of blossoms in the moonlight—posed no threat to me. I'm a big hulking boy, so says my girlfriend, and I don't have an imagination, so say most of my friends, so it took a while for me to identify the feeling that ran through me when I saw her. Unease. The tiny woman made me uncomfortable.

Or maybe the feeling was terror. My Saturn's headlights picked her out on the side of the road where she stood, and I was startled deep down in the pit of my stomach. I hit the brakes and swerved and the car stalled.

Road dust sprayed over the woman. I jumped out of the driver's seat red with embarrassment.

"I'm so sorry," I said. "Are you okay?" I was all right again, the fear a passing spasm that I ignored.

The woman laughed while she beat at her dark dress covered in tiny white dots and dust. "No need to worry, young man," she said. "I've been covered in worse. But I will take a ride." Without another word she opened the rear passenger door and slid into my car.

I hadn't meant to offer her a ride, but then I hadn't expected to see anyone up here on top of 22 Mountain. She was barefoot. Barefoot and walking on a mountain road at night, but she didn't look like a back-hollows girl: she had all her teeth and her skin was pearly white in the moonlight. A delicate scent of wild mountain freesia wafted from her. My grandma had worn that scent, *eau de flower* she called it, something she made up herself. This woman looked too delicate, too unworldly, to prepare her own scents. I bristled with curiosity: where'd she come from? How'd she get up here? But it's impolite to pry, my momma says, so I just settled back in the driver's seat and started up the car.

"Where are you headed?" she asked.

I looked at her reflection in the rear view mirror. Wasn't I supposed to ask her that question?

"Well, ma'am," I said, "I just concluded a little business transaction with some men up the hill, and now I'm on my way home to watch the Mountaineers play Pittsburgh on TV." I grinned. My girlfriend Ellie says it's a goofy grin. I hoped the woman would take the hint and not ask about the box full of quart mason jars in the passenger foot well. I should have put them in the trunk. "Where can I take you?"

She looked out the window and frowned. "Take me home, please."

"Yes, ma'am, and where's that?"

"Down to McConnell," she said. "Down to Logan Memorial Park."

That wasn't so far out of my way; I wouldn't be late for the game if I hurried. I didn't speed on the mountain road, of course; I'd make up the time when we got to the interstate. Only a suicide drives fast down a mountain at night.

She was quiet for a bit, in that high-pressure-storm-watch kind of way my girlfriend gets when she's about to yell at me. I tried to think of some chitchat that would defuse her mood, but I was too late.

"He traded me away for rent," she said. "Traded me to that awful banker who took me to his hunting lodge and used me like a whore."

I gulped. What could I possibly say?

She started singing a hymn, "Jesus Loves Me," and I have to say I liked her voice. Pretty and sweet and I bet she sang in the local church choir.

"Men don't like me, you know," she said. "They pretend to, until they get what they want. Women know better! I have *plenty* of women-friends."

"Ma'am, I'm sorry for your troubles," I said, "but I'm not sure these are secrets you should be sharing with me." I looked in my rear view mirror at her; she'd stopped mid-rant, her mouth hung open in shock like she'd been slapped.

"I mean. . . aren't these private things?"

"They murdered me," she said. "Should I keep that secret?"

"No, ma'am," I mumbled. *Oh boy. A nutcase.* "Maybe you should tell the cops. Murderers need to be locked up!"

She laughed, a little hysterical if you asked me.

"Locked up? Why, yes, my husband was locked up. Spent his whole retirement in the insane asylum," she said. She sounded pleased with that ending.

And a moment later she said, "Stomach cancer!"

Sometimes you just gotta keep your head down and keep pushing to the end. I'd promised her a ride, and I would get her to her destination, though I might not like it. I did notice the seat belt warning, and I ignored that as long as I could, but I had to speak up when we got to the onramp.

"Ma'am, we're at the interstate now," I said. "Would you please buckle your seat belt?"

"You keep mispronouncing my name," she said. Her voice had a faded quality, like a radio station that is almost out of range.

"I'm Mamie. Not ma'am."

"Yes, ma'am," I started to say but the words clung to the insides of my throat when I looked in the rear view mirror. She wasn't there.

I skidded to a stop, then thought better of stopping dead center on the interstate, and I drove to the verge and stopped again. I turned around and looked. She still wasn't in the back seat. I caught a whiff of her scent, wild mountain freesia, but that was all.

I don't have an imagination. I hadn't imagined the whole episode. And no regular person just up and disappears out of a car. This woman, Mamie, must have been a ghost. *Ipso facto*, right?

After the game I Googled what little I knew. *22 Mountain Road*: nothing. *Mamie*: far too many hits to read through. *22 Mountain Road* and *Mamie* together, plus *Logan Memorial Park*, and bingo.

Mamie Thurman had been murdered. Strangled, shot, throat slashed, discarded like so much trash on a mountain road. Only one person had stood trial, a black servant who'd died of stomach cancer. I shivered when I read that. The murder happened back in 1932, before my folks were born, maybe even before their folks had been born. The reports said a ghost had sometimes been seen on that mountain road, called Trace Mountain Road back then. But no reports said anything about conversations with the dead.

Maybe I was special.

Maybe not. But I thought maybe if I could see her again, I could help her find some peace.

In the thick of playoffs, I found an excuse to acquire more moonshine.

Last time I'd given the moonshiners some cash and shook hands all around and drove off, a bare minimum small talk. This time, I unscrewed the lid from a mason jar and took a sip of the crystal liquid inside. My nose started to burn. I held the jar out and they passed it along, each taking a healthy slug.

"So," I said. "The ghost."

The three brothers glanced at each other and broke into laughter. Locker-room laughter, thick with sniggering and innuendo. I thought I'd left that sound behind in high school.

"Old hot-to-trot Mamie!" Luke said. "Ha-cha-cha!"

"Hope she didn't touch you," Josh said. He looked at me sideways and spat some brown juice in a thin stream.

I shook my head.

"Hear tell she'll touch you just about any way you want, but you'll pay for it," said Malcolm. "Not money, what use has she got for money? But. . . Josh here," he pointed to the tobacco-chewing brother, "Josh used to be a good-lookin' man!"

They all laughed.

"Look, son," said Josh, "she's trouble. Don't you go lookin' for her. All the folks 'round these parts know better than to bother with her. She's trouble." He spat again.

I thanked them for their kindness and hauled the box of mason jars out to my car. This time I stowed them in the trunk.

I didn't think there was a chance in hell she'd be there, but she was. She stood prim on the side of the road, in the blue dress with white polka dots, her hair neatly styled and pinned up. She was beautiful; I hadn't dreamt that.

I stopped my Saturn and hopped out in time to grab the passenger door handle for her. "May I offer you a ride?" I said. I'd rehearsed the words.

She smiled at me and seated herself. I closed the door with

a quiet *snick*, not my usual *slam!*, then went around to the driver's side and got behind the wheel.

"Mrs. Thurman," I said, "may I take you home?"

She just smiled.

I drove without speaking, and she didn't say a word from the back seat. Her scent drifted up to me and maybe intoxicated me a little, because I swear the road changed from asphalt to dirt, and the trees looked thicker and older, and the car itself seemed to morph from my familiar Saturn to something boxier, some antique Ford maybe with bad springs and etched glass windows. I glanced at the tiny rear view mirror when the car touched the interstate but didn't insist on a seat belt this time.

She didn't disappear.

The trip to McConnell was fast, fast as I could accelerate and not get pulled over by the lurking police. The utter silence from the back seat scared me; I never was scared before, but now I feared to look in the rear view mirror at whatever the ghost of Mamie Thurman might have become. My underused imagination worked overtime, filling in with images from TV and the movies: she'd have turned into a ragged green skeletal thing, dripping ooze, or perhaps a vampire-like beast with intestines hanging out and blood everywhere. I felt cold all right, but was it from the ghost in the back seat or from my own unfamiliar terror screaming at me to stop the car and get out?

Soon I found McConnell and the entrance to Logan Memorial Park. I dared a glance at the woman in my back seat.

She sat there, her hands primly folded in her lap. She held a cotton and lace handkerchief; it was rumpled and damp, as if she'd been sobbing and wiping her face with it.

"We're here," I said. "Logan Memorial Park." A dirt turn-out stretched ahead. The cemetery lay at the end of the dirt road, about a hundred yards up.

I climbed out of my car and discovered it was indeed a rickety old Ford, spindly tires and dust-covered matte black paint job. A stone triple-arch that hadn't been there a moment ago spanned the dirt turn-out to the cemetery. I opened the passenger door (not so easily; those old cars had different handles and I'd never used one before) and waited while Mrs. Thurman stepped out.

Her smile was predatory. "How can I *repay* your kindness to me?" she said.

I shook my head. "I'm happy to help."

"Nonsense. All the men want *something* from me. A kiss perhaps?" She moved a little closer to me, and I have to admit I jumped backwards.

"Oh no, ma'am, thank you anyway," I stammered. My hands were sweating. "My. . . Ellie, my girlfriend, is so jealous, she'd never understand."

Mrs. Thurman gave me a fleeting smile. "I just can't tell about you," she said. "You treat your girlfriend right, you hear me?"

She turned and walked under the stone arch, her bare feet lifting little pads of dust. In a moment she was lost in the fields among the headstones and flowering vines.

I breathed. My car was once again a shiny black Saturn, 2004 model with cloth upholstery. I was never so glad to see it in my life. I settled back in the driver's seat. The turnout to Logan Memorial Park was once again the dreary forgotten road, the stone arch faded away.

My girlfriend found it the next day, a spot of white on the

black seat.

"Fred, where'd you get this?" she said. Ellie opened the bit of cotton and lace up and I caught a whiff of wild mountain freesia. "This is a woman's handkerchief. Who do you know with the initials MT?"

I eased the hanky away from her. Hard as it was, I never did share that story with her. Some things are best kept private.

ACKNOWLEDGEMENTS

— This anthology would not be possible without the writers who went beyond the call of duty in making this project a special one. I am in awe at the level of professionalism and pride each of you exude.

— Thanks to Keith and Cheryl Davis at *Woodland Press* for having the determination to see this project through and in print. Thanks for allowing me to be a part of it.

— Thanks to Rick Hautala for taking valuable work time and writing a terrific foreword. After speaking with the governor, we are making you an honorary West Virginian.

— Thanks to Gary A. Braunbeck, James Gunn, Laura Benedict, Mary Sangiovanni, and Fran Friel for the wonderful words and friendship.

— Thanks to Matt at *Shocklines*, Larry at *Bloodletting Books*, Dan,

Susan, and the whole gang at *The Other Dark Place, Cat At The Red Light District,* and Nanci at *Horror World* for allowing me to spam your message boards with announcements about this project.

— Thanks to Jerry Jones for the beautiful cover art. You are one *amazing* individual.

— Thanks to my *lovely* wife Jewell (aptly named by the way) for putting up with the late hours, the mood swings, and the mass quantities of Jello Pudding. *Love, love, love* . . .

Other Fine Titles By Woodland Press, LLC

The Tale Of The Devil:
The Biography of Devil Anse Hatfield

Dr. Coleman C. Hatfield and Robert Y. Spence
(Dr. Hatfield was named Tamarack Author of the Year in 2004)

The Secret Life and Brutal Death
Of Mamie Thurman

By F. Keith Davis

West Virginia Tough Boys
Vote Buying, Fist Fighting And A President Named JFK

By F. Keith Davis

Mountain Boy
The Adventures of Orion Saddler

By Norman Mullins

Prickett's Fort

By Bill Hawkins

... and many others ...

www.woodlandpress.com

BOOK RESELLERS / BOOKSTORES:
If you'd like to carry *Woodland Press* book titles, contact:

West Virginia Book Company

Telephone (888)-982-7472
1125 Central Avenue , Charleston WV 25302
(www.wvbookco.com) e-mail: wvbooks@verizon.net

Or, contact *Woodland Press, LLC* directly, (304) 752-7152; FAX 304-752-9002; 118 Woodland Dr., Suite 1101, Chapmanville, WV 25508; e-mail: info@woodland-press.com; or BookWorld Distributors, www.bookworld.com.

Michael Knost is an author, editor, and publisher of horror fiction and resides in Logan, West Virginia. He has written several books, tons of short stories, and a few nonfiction columns.

He is also the publisher of *Noctem Aeternus,* a new free quarterly PDF magazine (see page 160) focusing on science fiction, fantasy, western and mystery stories ...*but all tales with an element of horror.*

Noctem Aeternus incudes stories from some of the giants of the industry, such as Ramsey Campbell, Cherie Priest, Charles Coleman Finlay, Tim Waggoner, and Michael Laimo. Interviews are also included by writers, artists and personalities like Ramsey Campbell, Rob Zombie, Kuang Hong and others.

When it seems like every genre anthology released these days tries to convince readers that it and it alone is reinventing the wheel, *Legends of the Mountain State: Ghostly Tales from the State of West Virginia* is more than a breath of fresh air; it's a testament to the power of traditional, simple story-telling. Editor Michael Knost has assembled thirteen elegant, eerie, and affecting ghost stories written by authors who know and respect the tradition of such tales, and each offers up an atmospheric, straightforward, uncluttered narrative that one can easily imagine being told around a campfire late at night, as the stars blink down their light from a cold heaven and the sounds beyond the fire become unnervingly semi-human. There is poetic elegance in such simplicity, and this outstanding anthology proves it over and again. *Simply superb*."

— Gary A. Braunbeck

Bram Stoker and International Horror Guild Award-winner, and author of The Cedar Hill Stories and Mr. Hands

REVISED SECOND EDITION

The
Secret Life
and
Brutal Death
of
Mamie
Thurman

F. KEITH DAVIS

Thurman, Mamie 21 June 1932

Woodland Press and Quarrier Press Present

The Secret Life and Brutal Death
Of Mamie Thurman

This mysterious true story of a brutal homicide is now available for order.

1932 Chilling Mamie Thurman murder case reexamined

CHARLESTON, WV – Seventy-five years ago, in the cradle of southern West Virginia's most rugged mountain range, a bizarre murder grabbed national headlines, due to the peculiar circumstances surrounding the gruesome homicide. Now, a book — a new revision offering greater detail and newly discovered information — takes another look at this puzzling account, which involved a number of white-collar suspects, an intense community scandal and a shocking gangland-style execution that still baffles the public.

A full re-write and revision of a former literary hit, *The Secret Life and Brutal Death of Mamie Thurman*, is now available and is published by Quarrier Press, of Charleston, in collaboration with Woodland Press, LLC. The volume represents the first in-depth work about Logan County, West Virginia socialite Mamie Thurman and her inexplicable, gruesome murder in 1932. It includes several all-new chapters in the murder case.

In spite of this woman's local notoriety and the fact that her husband was a respected City of Logan police officer at the time, Mamie was savagely destroyed on a rainy night in June — shot in the head; neck fractured; face disfigured; throat cut; and her lifeless corpse dumped over a mountainside, like garbage at an illegal dump site.

The composition, authored by newspaperman and Logan County resident F. Keith Davis, is a bone-chilling examination of the slaying that now includes new photograph evidence from the original state police investigation and actual court testimony from the subsequent trial, which revealed the murdered woman's adulterous affairs with several prominent local businessmen.

According to Bill Clements, of Quarrier Press, "This new work is a complete reconsideration of its predecessor. It includes much more research and interview material than its former release. There are also several new chapters that better cover the decades-old case. The author grabs the reader's attention from the onset. It's part crime drama, part rollercoaster ride, and most amazing of all, this is a true story. Such a riveting literary work should be in every home and high school/college library across the state."

"The magnitude of this appalling scandal cannot be imagined unless understood within the framework of its time period and locality," said Davis, the author. "It was a terribly immoral and violent report from the heart of the Bible belt during the last year of Prohibition. And since 1932, the story has taken on urban legend status, where there are claims of ghostly sightings of the murder victim and other weird occurrences that are documented every year."

Even today, there are some who say that on a still night the tormented voice of Mamie Thurman's ghost echoes through the trees and across the mountains near Holden, WV, crying out for truth, justice and closure, though chances for lasting peace seem most unlikely.

"Due to its subject matter, and the historic research involved in this venture, I think this book is destined to become a true cult-classic," Clements added. "We encourage readers to contact us via e-mail once they've read the book, to give us their take on the criminal case. Help us solve the mystery that still surrounds Mamie Thurman's ugly and abrupt death."

The author, Keith Davis, who has been interviewed on C-Span BookTV and featured on many radio and television programs over the years, is also the writer of *West Virginia Tough Boys*, another West Virginia bestseller, published by Woodland Press, about the making of, and the behind-the-scenes shenanigans related to, some of the best-known Mountain State politicians of yesteryear.

The completely revised edition of *The Secret Life and Brutal Death of Mamie Thurman* is a bone-chilling companion book with *Legends Of The Mountain State,* and is available at better bookstores everywhere. For more information, contact Quarrier Press, by phone, 304-342-1848; or by email: wvbooks@verizon.net or, woodlandpressllc@mac.com.

Free Subscription